A Curious

Wedding

Plus
A Finn Family Christmas

The Finn Factor, Book 5

R.G. ALEXANDER

A Curious Wedding

Copyright © 2016 R.G. Alexander

Formatted by IRONHORSE Formatting

ISBN: 1725821850
ISBN-13: 978-1725821859

Dedication

I will never be able to thank the Finn Factor fans and Finn Club readers enough for their patience, support and love for these characters. In my mind, you embody all the best qualities of our favorite family and I'm so glad to have you on this journey with me.
This little Christmas story is all for you.

And to Cookie—Love is the reason.
Now more than ever.

Shawn and Ellen Finn
are proud to announce the
wedding of their son

Owen Finn

to

Jeremy Porter

This Christmas Eve,
join the Finn family as we
celebrate the blessed season
with the greatest blessing
of all. Love.

CHAPTER ONE

Owen Finn

2 days to Christmas Eve…

Owen Finn was having one hell of a good dream. Or—he smiled inwardly when the sound of his own moans made his heavy eyelids lift—his favorite kind of wake up call.

"Mmm. Morning." He watched Jeremy through his lashes and tangled his fingers in mussed dark hair, each tug of his lover's mouth setting small fireworks off through his body. "Is it Christmas?"

Jeremy's mouth was too occupied to answer.

Owen's teeth scraped across his lower lip and he

rocked his hips as his cock disappeared down the talented throat of his fiancé. "Fuck, never mind. Will you still do this after the wedding, or do I need to add it to the vows? Do you, Jeremy Porter, promise to love, honor, obey me anytime I ask you to suck my dick?"

Jeremy let Owen's cock slide out from between his lips to fall heavy and hard on his belly. He climbed up the bed and kissed Owen's chin. "You can *not* add that."

"That sounds like a dare." His low laugh morphed into a surprised groan as cold lube slipped between the cheeks of his ass, swiftly followed by Jeremy's talented fingers. "Wait. I want that mouth back on my—Oh Jesus, that's good." He bent his knees and spread his legs wide, gasping raggedly when two large fingers pushed inside. "God, it must be Christmas. I don't know what I did but it looks like I've been a damn good boy."

Jeremy skimmed Owen's lips with his own as he thrust deep, hitting his prostate with every stroke. God he had talented hands. Artist's hands. "Good isn't the word I'd use," he whispered hotly. "In fact, I see a lump of coal in your future, because you've been a giant pain in my ass."

Owen bit down on Jeremy's lower lip. "As often as possible," he agreed, breathless. "And you love it."

4

Desperate sounds escaped his throat as Jeremy looked into his eyes without a word while he stretched his ass. It was intimate and powerful, and it took all of Owen's willpower not to beg.

He was slowly coming to terms with how little control he had with Jeremy. The need was too consuming and it never faded. Never eased. Owen reached down to grasp the big, brutally large cock he loved and gripped as much of it as he could. "You planning on returning the favor this morning, big guy? I could take that kind of pain in my ass all day."

Jeremy grit his teeth and his fingers plunged deeper, making Owen gasp. "Oh I will, Owen. But you know that's not what I mean."

"I know you want me. You always want me."

"I do."

"Get used to saying that." Owen's hips were restless, practically lifting his body off the bed when Jeremy started to pump faster, harder. A thumb grazed his tight balls and he shuddered. "I swear as soon as the wedding is over I'm going to take you back to our cabin and consummate the hell out of your ass if you don't fuck me right now."

"That's not exactly a threat." Jeremy's breath panted

against his lips, close enough for a kiss. "After all you've put me through the last few months, I should make you wait. Torture you the way you love to torture me."

"You know what happens once it's my turn." *I'll tie you up and paddle your ass until you're shouting for release. I'll make you do the begging. And then I'll bury myself inside you until we both get what we want. Until neither one of us can walk.*

The visual only made him hotter. "Fuck me."

"Say please."

"*Please, damn it.*"

Jeremy moved in between his thighs like a warrior claiming his spoils. He was fucking glorious. He'd grown his beard back for the wedding at Owen's request, and between that, all his muscles and the stunning Maori tattoos on his ass and thighs, Jeremy looked fierce. A predator. In this moment he wasn't the buddy who'd let him cheat off his papers in high school, or got drunk with him when he snuck bottles out of his father's pub and lounged around playing videogames instead of meeting his deadline, just because Owen was bored.

An angel in the streets, a wild man in the sheets, and mine every day, Owen thought proudly, knowing it was true. Jeremy Porter—soon to be Porter-Finn—was his best friend, his heart and, whenever the mood struck them, a willing submissive that could take whatever Owen dished out. But he wasn't submitting now. At the moment he was coating his monster erection with lube, his hard gaze daring Owen to stop him.

He never would. It didn't matter what he'd thought he wanted before. What kink he'd called his own or what his sexuality used to be. His orientation was Jeremy. All he wanted was Jeremy. Anything and everything they did together felt right.

Right and too damn slow. "Stop showing off," he demanded, shamelessly gripping his thighs and lifting them so his ass was spread and on display. "I need that big fucking cock inside me."

"You are a cocky, shameless bastard." Jeremy groaned and guided himself inside. Owen's body shook with that first, forceful thrust. The stretch was so good. He was so full he saw stars.

"Yes. That's it. God, that's what I want. All of it. Don't you fucking stop. Give the bastard what he deserves."

His knees pressed against his chest as Jeremy kept sinking deeper, stretching him almost to the point of pain and giving him exactly what he asked for. Every thick, delicious inch. Owen blew out a rough breath and took more, his eyes nearly rolling back in his head from the raw pleasure.

All of it. All of you, Jeremy. All mine.

Jeremy's expression was tight, his cheeks ruddy when their bodies finally pressed flush against each other. "Owen." That one word was so full of lust and love and need that he couldn't resist lifting up, cupping the back of Jeremy's head and pulling him down for a deep, carnal kiss.

Love you so much.

"I want this to last," Jeremy grunted as he started to roll his hips, his cock so deep that Owen could hardly breathe. "I want to *make* this last."

"Later," he promised, biting Jeremy's neck in a way that made the bigger man shiver. "Much later. For our thirtieth anniversary we can go slow. Maybe by then you'll be able to resist my sexy ass." *Not if I have anything to say about it.* "I don't want slow and easy now. I want to ache every time I sit down tomorrow, and I want to finish inside *your* ass."

Jeremy made a ragged sound Owen took as agreement, pulling back and starting a hard rhythm that had them both shouting in ecstasy.

Yes. Fucking me so hard. Love you.

Owen's erection was dripping and painfully hard but he bit his lip until he tasted blood and held back. Jeremy claimed him again and again, his muscular body straining over him. *Not yet.* "Come, Jeremy. Give it to me."

He let go of the flexing body above him, his body on fire and his lungs struggling for every breath as he searched the bed for the bottle of lube. When he found it he opened it and poured a liberal amount on his dick, watching Jeremy's eyes darken.

Owen stroked himself, coating his heated flesh and hissing as the sensation nearly made his cock explode. "This is for you," he growled. "As soon as you let go I'm going to get you on your knees and fuck you into this mattress."

He didn't want him to stop, but the way Jeremy reacted to his promise was too satisfying. His hips jerked and his rhythm sped up, the sound of their skin slapping against each other filling their bedroom. "Fuck," Owen gasped, gripping the base of his shaft. "That's so good. Keep doing that and I'll lose it. I'll have to fuck you with your second favorite toy until I'm ready for round two. I know you love it but it won't be as goo—"

"*Christ.*"

Jeremy came with a shout. Warmth filled Owen's ass and dripped down his ass cheeks, and he shivered when the still-hard shaft slid out of him.

"My turn." Owen didn't hesitate, flipping the trembling Jeremy onto his stomach and gripping his hips. "On your knees," he ordered roughly. "I can't wait."

"Owen," Jeremy moaned, obeying him instantly. "Please."

"You don't have to beg. I know what you need." Owen slid one hand up Jeremy's back until he was cupping his head, pressing it into the mattress. "Keep your hands on the bed or I'll stop and get the handcuffs. And I don't want to stop. Do you understand?"

"Yes," Jeremy moaned, still breathing hard from his release. "Yes, Owen."

They both gasped when he guided his cock deep inside. "Good," he sighed. "So good. Yeah that's exactly what I need."

He couldn't talk anymore. Couldn't think. All he could do was focus on holding back long enough to make Jeremy wild. He found the perfect angle and used all of his control, pounding into him over and over with unerring accuracy while Jeremy cried out his name in desperation and desire.

Owen knew his body. His big, insatiable cock was erect again, and Owen knew exactly what it would take to get it to do what he wanted. *Come again for me. Show me who you belong to.*

All he could hear was his heart pulsing in his ears and the faint, continuous sounds of pleasure coming from the man beneath him as he brought him closer to his second climax. He saw Jeremy's fists clench in the sheets and gripped his wrist, needing to touch him. He pulled one arm behind his back and pushed his face further into the soft bed they shared. "You're there, aren't you?" Owen rasped. "Ready to come with me?"

Jeremy's shout of affirmation was muffled, but full-throated. Owen was addicted to this high. The more he demanded, the more it turned Jeremy on. He'd never let go like that for anyone else. Never given that kind of trust.

Only to me.

They were both so close. It took all of his will to hold back until he heard Jeremy's hoarse cry and felt his ass clenching around him before he let go and joined him in a release that ripped through his spine and down his cock, taking everything until he was completely spent.

He released his grip on Jeremy and fell over him. Chest to back, racing hearts slowing together, Owen tried to remember what sex was like before this, but it wasn't worth the brain cells. Everything else paled and faded in comparison. As far as he was concerned, they invented sex and should at least get a federal holiday named after them. Or a trophy. Something.

He heard a high-pitched whine. "Shit, the dog." Owen kissed Jeremy's shoulder and sighed regretfully. "You start the shower, I'll let Badass out before he takes a leak on the carpet."

"Don't forget to put on his booties. It snowed last night."

Owen snorted, rolling his eyes as he stood on shaky legs and walked the large dog down the hall and toward the back balcony doors. "Fucking booties, man. You don't really need them, do you? Your name is *Badass*. You're covered in fur and fearlessness." He unlocked the glass door and slid it open. "Your ancestors were roaming the—*son of a motherfucking witches*—" He slammed the door shut again as Badass whined. "I think my dick just relocated to a warmer climate. How about you, buddy?"

Owen grabbed the blanket folded on the back of the couch and wrapped it around himself like a cocoon. "Let's get those damn booties on and get this over with."

Luckily Badass was in no mood to linger after doing his business. He didn't even go down the stairs, but he still came back in covered in wet snow. "Shake it off," Owen told him. "We don't need puddles of melting dog all over the house." Badass gave himself a shake and Owen winced as the hard drops hit him like tiny ice missiles. He couldn't blame him for whining and shivering. If he had to go out in that every time he needed to piss, he'd be shaking in his booties too.

Just thinking about it made him... "Damn it."

He tossed his blanket over the grateful dog and then raced into the bathroom. Jeremy was already under the steaming hot spray when Owen ran in to use the toilet. "I think we should get Badass a jacket to match his booties. Or teach him how to go in the guest bathroom."

Jeremy's laugh drifted through the steam and made him smile. "That cold, huh?"

"That cold. I hope Freddy is delivering, because we're not going anywhere today." Owen stepped under the spray and into Jeremy's arms, shivering and hissing as the hot water landed on his icy extremities. "On second thought, maybe I could settle for whatever's in the fridge. I don't want him to suffer this kind of pain. He's got that bad knee and frostbite is a real danger for delivery men this time of year."

"My Good Samaritan," Jeremy murmured, kissing his neck. "The only man I know who gets a Christmas card from a pizza place."

His beard scraped, reminding Owen of the first time they kissed and how he'd made him shave. He wasn't going to tell him how much he liked it now. How he loved seeing the marks on his skin and feeling the sting of beard burn after a long session of loving. If he did, he wouldn't get the joy of shaving him during their honeymoon. And he'd been practicing. It was the first thing on his to do list after tying him up.

"They do love me there," Owen agreed, tilting his head. "And my cravings keep them in business. Now wash me and warm me, and then we'll eat something and spend the rest of the day in bed."

Jeremy was noticeably silent as he soaped Owen's body thoroughly. By the time he rinsed him off, Owen was breathing heavily and toasty warm. He reached for him for another round, but Jeremy stepped out of the shower and away from his touch, avoiding eye contact.

Shit. "What did I do?"

Jeremy sighed, shaking his head as he dried himself off. "I'm trying to decide if you're doing this on purpose or if you really forgot."

Owen shut off the water, his mood disappearing with the heated spray. "I didn't forget. I was enjoying the momentary hope that you would."

He *had* forgotten for a few minutes. Waking up with your cock in someone's mouth had a tendency to cause temporary amnesia. But time was ticking by and there was no avoiding it now. Today was the day he'd been dreading for weeks. And nothing he said or did would change Jeremy's mind on the subject.

He was leaving.

"This is stupid," Owen repeated for the hundredth time as Jeremy handed him a towel. "Superstitious bullshit invented to stop men from running away if they didn't think their future bride was as hot as her dowry. I already know you're hot and we can plainly see that I'm irresistible. No one's running anywhere, so just *stay with me.*"

Jeremy looked as tempted as he always did, but also just as determined. "It's traditional. And you'll be too distracted to notice I'm gone. Brady's sending Rory, Noah and Wyatt here to stay with you for the duration."

"Notice he didn't offer," Owen muttered. And why would he? He had a nice bed and a sexy, willing man who didn't want to sleep anywhere else.

"He'll be at the pub for the bachelor party. Then you'll have a day to recover so you aren't hung over for the wedding, and that's it. It'll fly by."

Owen slammed his hand on the doorframe, blocking Jeremy's escape. "I'll notice that my best friend isn't at my bachelor party. I'll notice that my fiancé isn't in our bed when I fall into it drunk off my ass and needing a blowjob."

Jeremy forced a chuckle, but he was obviously frustrated. "Your best friend *has* to miss that after-party blowjob so he can marry you on Christmas Eve, you stubborn jackass. Don't you think I'd rather hang out with the guys? Your sister keeps texting me with pictures of penis candy and bridal tiaras. She and Tasha have been exchanging dirty Christmas lyrics on my phone, most of them revolving around the size of my—" He shook his head. "That's what *I* have to put up with for the next few days. For you. So man up and stop being difficult."

Owen frowned. "I'm never difficult."

"Are you kidding me?" Jeremy pushed through Owen's barricade and headed for his dresser, letting his towel fall so he could step into his black briefs. Owen couldn't help but admire his song-worthy semi before he covered it up. "You changed the wedding date—twice. You kept changing your mind about locations and decorations and food. If Jen's professor hadn't offered us the use of his…what do you call a house that big?"

"A shopping mall?" Owen muttered, though he secretly wanted to house swap for that media wall alone. "I still don't know how he lived by himself for so long. No single person needs that much space. Our whole family could live there. Tanaka has money too, you don't see him flaunting it." Or having a threesome with the littlest Finn.

Jeremy rolled his eyes. "That may look like one loft, Owen, but you know Ken owns the entire building he and Brady are living in. He just has elevators instead of a grand staircase. And don't start. You love that house. Getting married there was your call and you can't change your mind again or I might get violent."

Owen couldn't argue with that. "It's a great house and I'm not changing my mind. Everything's settled, I promise. It all worked out in the end."

"Not before you almost gave your mother an anxiety disorder and me a permanent migraine. But this is where I'm drawing the line. From now on we're going traditional. Or, as traditional as we can be. That means no sleeping together or seeing each other before the wedding, bachelor parties and reception dances and every damn thing people do to celebrate the biggest day of their lives." Jeremy paused, his lips quirking. "In deference to you, Declan has already attached the game system to his magical television wall—which will only come on *after* you've danced with me and taken a few wedding pictures for your mother's sake."

"And then we fuck each other's brains out?"

"Yes, Mr. Romance. And then—till we're parted by death—we fuck each other's brains out."

"You know the way to my heart." Owen reached for the waistband of Jeremy's briefs, letting his towel drop as he pulled him closer. "I'm sorry I've been off." Jeremy raised his eyebrow. "Fine. I've been batshit crazy, okay? To be fair, since the proposal everyone's been a little insane about our wedding. Mom kept trying to make it what *she* thought it should be, reporters started showing up at my construction sites talking about the effect our engagement was having on Stephen's poll numbers, and you were always so busy. I was…well, I'm—"

"Spoiled rotten? Used to getting your way and having all the attention? A domineering pain in the ass?"

"Exactly." Owen's lips twitched. "I'm only planning on doing this once, you know. Is it wrong that I wanted to get it right?"

Jeremy wrapped his arms around him and pressed their foreheads together. "As long as you show up, it's going to be right."

"I'm the one who proposed, of course *I'm* showing up. And the only reason I'm letting you out of my sight is because Tasha is pregnant. If she weren't still working full time on her twin project, I'd be afraid she'd slip something in your drink and drive you to Canada to have one last ménage with her and some skinny screamer who doesn't deserve you."

Jeremy snorted. "She'd never do that, Owen. And not just because she's married to Stephen and too pregnant to see her feet. She loves you and she's the only one who's always known how I felt about you. Next to your mother, no one is happier about our wedding than she is. Though she is pissed about that wheelchair."

Owen caressed the broad shoulders in front of him. Stephen mentioned something about Natasha's head exploding when he told her the only way she could be Jeremy's *best woman* was on wheels.

He'd offered to postpone everything until the babies were born, but his confident, politically savvy older brother had paled and begged him not to mention it again. She would, according to him, make him suffer in ways Owen couldn't imagine if the wedding date was changed because of her. He didn't ask for details. But knowing Tasha, he could imagine. "How is she really? You went with them to the checkup yesterday, but you didn't go into detail."

"You didn't give me a lot of time for talking when I got home," Jeremy said with a small smirk. "But yeah, I went. I guess Rory decided to come before his shift because he was there too. She's experiencing intense mood swings, but the doctor said that's perfectly normal. He told us she's almost eight months, but the twins are growing fast now, which is good. They're not going to wait any longer than they have to for the C-section. It could be as soon as two weeks." Jeremy's worried expression had Owen holding him tighter instinctively.

The sooner the better, as far as Owen was concerned.

"And we will spoil those kids rotten to pay her back for all the trouble she's gotten us into since high school. I just wish she'd tell us the sex so I could start planning all my *Cool Uncle* presents."

Jeremy nuzzled Owen's neck, his lips skimming flesh as he responded. "She ordered the doctor not to tell them, and to only give them sonogram pictures that aren't revealing. He's obviously more afraid of her than a sitting senator, because he's not talking. She wants it to be a surprise."

He'd lost his train of thought. Lips on his neck and that beard scraping his skin was all it took to distract him. God, he was so easy. Owen leaned back against the doorframe, dragging Jeremy's hips against his renewed erection. "When do you have to leave again?"

"As soon as you let me go," Jeremy mumbled, as distracted now as he was. "Ken and Little Finn are joining us at Tasha's for the evening. Stephen's only rule is that she doesn't lift a finger."

Owen frowned. "Tanaka's going to be there? Why?"

"Tasha invited him. Partially so I wouldn't be the only guy, I think, but it's probably not the only reason. She wants to find out what's going on with their never-ending investigation. She's worried about Brady since

21

Jen told her what he had Trick doing."

He remembered Trick's battered face after he'd helped his cousin, and he felt like a prick because he didn't care as much about that as he did the presence of Tanaka at Jeremy's slumber party. But he snuffed out the small spark of jealousy fast enough. Kenneth Tanaka was in love with Brady, and he was a friend. An attractive, tattooed friend who was masterful with rope and would be spending time with Jeremy when Owen wasn't allowed to.

He moved swiftly. Hands in Jeremy's hair, tugging until their lips met, he walked him back toward the bed. He lifted his mouth before pushing Jeremy roughly onto the mattress. "You don't have to be in such a rush. Bend over the bed."

Jeremy started to resist but whatever he saw in Owen's expression made him turn without a word and bend over.

"Knees on the mattress," Owen ordered. "Now."

He smiled at the sight of Jeremy's cotton-covered ass in the air, massaging the cheeks with firm hands. Lowering the briefs until they stretched taut around thickly muscled thighs he sighed, his mouth watering. "You're not going anywhere until I kiss you goodbye."

He heard the ragged moan of submission and bent down, lids heavy as he licked his lips.

"Owen?" A familiar male voice called down the hallway, accompanied by his dog's excited barks. *A little late on triggering the alarm, Badass.* "The cool kids have arrived."

Noah. *Son of a bitch.*

Jeremy swore too and rolled away with impressive speed, yanking his briefs up and reaching for his jeans. His expression was pained as he forced his huge erection safely behind his zipper. "Your family has great timing. Get dressed Owen."

A laugh—this time from a different Finn who was a little too close for comfort. "Yeah get dressed Owen," Rory called loudly from just outside the door. "We don't need to see the family jewels. Though I wouldn't mind getting a peek at Porter's."

"This is why we don't take you anywhere," Wyatt intoned from somewhere behind him. "No sense of personal space."

"Or decency," Noah added. "Stop perving on your cousin's husband."

"Like you two know about personal space. Don't firemen sleep together?" Rory's voice was fading, but

23

his mischievous tone was pissing Owen off. "Anyway, they aren't married yet, and I hear he's hung like a bull. I was just curious."

Jeremy and Owen's eyes met at that and held, remembering. Jeremy smiled before reaching into the dresser and throwing Owen's favorite sweatpants in his direction. "Come on. Walk me to the door."

His fiancé picked up his stuffed gym bag and a winter jacket. Owen knew both of their wedding tuxedos were already pressed and hanging at Declan's house, and all the other details in Jeremy's wedding binder were checked off and taken care of. There'd be no reason for him to come back before the big event. "Badass is going to miss you."

Jeremy turned and walked backwards down the hallway. "As long as he doesn't get drunk on beer again or throw up all over the couch because you left takeout containers on the coffee table, he'll live. He won't even notice I'm gone."

"He'll notice." *I'll notice.* "If Tasha hires a stripper I'm writing her out of the will."

His smile was telling. "You think the Senator's wife—who is currently an invalid propped up on pillows with two buns in one oven—is going to invite a male stripper into her home to give me a lap dance?"

Owen's glare was pointed. "Yes."

"I'm not saying she wouldn't." Jeremy held up his hands, conceding. "But if she did no one told me about it. Maybe she'll just have Ken do one of his rope demos for us. In this family, that's practically G-rated."

"He'll answer to me if he does."

Jeremy tsked. "So you get to have all the fun, is that what you're saying? Is this what marriage is going to be like with you? What's good for the goose isn't good for the other goose?"

Noah, already sprawled on the couch with a gaming controller in his hand, snorted loudly, drawing Owen's gaze. Wyatt was carrying four six-packs to the kitchen and Rory was rolling around on the floor with the dog. He shook his head and turned back to Jeremy. "Please don't leave me alone with these children, goose. I'll strip for you right here."

"Please don't." Rory sat up, wiping his dog-kissed face with a grin. "And stop being such a baby. The four biggest troublemakers of the family are together without adult supervision. It sounds like a party to me."

Jeremy hesitated. "You're in charge, Noah. Don't make me regret it. If you end up in jail or Owen doesn't make it to the wedding? You'll be responsible."

Noah didn't look away from the screen, but his easy nod made his short blond curls bounce. "You got it, Porter. Now go get your freak on with Team Jeremy. I hear the stripper they got for you dresses like a construction worker and he's packing a socket wrench that rivals your own."

"What?" Rory frowned at Noah's head. "Can I change teams?"

"Thought you did that years ago." Wyatt cracked himself up.

Noah smirked. "Too late. You're staying with us for the duration. We're with the groom."

"But—"

"No, Rory." Noah and Wyatt responded together, making Jeremy laugh.

Owen let him pull him to the door, away from his cousins. "Relax. I'm sure his socket wrench has nothing on yours," Jeremy assured him, his expression softening. "But I really do have to go if we're going to pull this off by Christmas Eve."

They came together for a kiss that went from gentle and loving to breathless and erotic in a heartbeat. All Owen could think about was finishing where they left off before they were interrupted. But when the catcalls and helpful hints from his cousins got louder, he lifted his lips with a sigh. "Does this traditional separation allow phone calls?"

"I'll call you tonight." Jeremy lifted the collar of his jacket against the snow and slipped out the door quickly, trying not to let too much cold air inside. "Love you."

Owen shivered, still shirtless as the door closed behind him. "Me too."

CHAPTER TWO

"This is bad." Wyatt's comment made Owen turn away from the door.

"What?"

"I don't know what the man-love equivalent of pussy-whipped is—"

"Dick-smacked?" Rory threw out helpfully. "Dong-flogged?"

"Thanks." Wyatt smirked. "The favored son of the house of Finn is officially dick-smacked. Staring at the door like you haven't been living in each other's back pockets for most of your lives. Like you're not going to see him day after tomorrow." He shook his head. "You used to be a player, buddy. A legend. I never saw it coming."

"I know," Rory sighed mournfully. "We were the dynamic duo. Now I'm the only legend left."

"Did you say *only*?" Wyatt sounded offended.

"Being in a calendar doesn't make you a legend, Wyatt. Just photogenic."

"I can show you legend."

"Please don't take off your shirt again."

"Enough you two." Noah paused the game, grabbed a beer from his brother and turned on the couch to face them. "And don't be too hard on dick-smacked over there. He didn't see it coming either. Frankly, I'm not sure he's ready for Christmas Eve. Our golden boy fears change, and this is about as big as it gets."

Owen crossed his arms and shook his head. "*I* fear change? *Me*? I can't believe you're saying that with a straight face. I damn well paved the way for the rest of you. You can fall in love with a dick-fingered Martian if you want and no one will bat an eye. Don't mock me. Thank me."

"First of all, that sounds like a good idea for a sci-fi porn, but technically? Big brother Brady did the paving," Rory corrected. "He was a giant gay Marine before it was cool. And then I came out in high school… Jeremy was bisexual pretty much from the get-go, right? Why exactly should we be thanking you again?"

Owen glowered at his cousin's facts. "You came out but no one else came in. You've never brought anyone home to meet the family."

"Sol's a homophobe and Jeremy was practically adopted by your parents already," Rory countered. "Doesn't count. Anyway, Brady did it for me after your proposal. Don't steal your best man's thunder. Give my brother his due."

Owen rolled his eyes. "Fine, Brady is the paver. He's also the only one of you who stepped off the path Sol the Elder laid out for his sons."

"Also not true," Wyatt said, pretending to be insulted. "I'm a fireman. He wanted us all to be cops."

Solomon and James were police officers, but these three were still first responders. Two cops, two firemen and an EMT. Brady *had* been a police officer, then a Marine, a politician's bodyguard and now...well, Owen wasn't sure what to call him now. He was still fighting criminals by working with Ken, so he hadn't wandered too far from the master plan.

Rory stood and wiped the dog hair off his shirt. "He wanted us all to date women, too. To be fruitful with the multiplying and not mar the family name."

Noah choked on his beer and chuckled. "Poor old Sol. Nothing ever goes his way."

Wyatt grinned. "Well *we're* not gay." He checked with Noah. "We're not, right? Not that it would matter to me if you decided to hop the fence but..."

"As far as I know. But now I'm worried you've been breathing in too many of those bad fumes again." Noah shook his head. "It doesn't matter. Sol blusters about family reputation, but caring about us personally is a little outside of his capabilities."

"Oh he cares," Rory muttered to no one in particular. "Just not in the way you'd want him to."

"That intervention did a number on him, didn't it?" Wyatt whistled as if to convey a bomb dropping. "The look on his face when we told him we knew about his ménage with Ellen and Uncle Shawn? I've never seen him like that. I guess he thought he'd get to the grave with that secret."

"I wish I'd been a fly on the wall." Owen was damn proud of his cousins for confronting Sol. They'd all needed to get a few things off their chest. "I can't believe he didn't pop a blood vessel."

"I was on hand for that, just in case," Rory assured him dryly. "But the old man is resilient, if nothing else."

31

Noah shook his head. "I don't know if it did any good. He is who he is, and one honest conversation isn't going to change that. I hope Uncle Shawn isn't disappointed when he doesn't show up for the wedding."

"I know he's grateful you tried. Despite it all, Dad still misses his twin. I can't imagine Stephen and Seamus being angry at each other for that long."

"How is Seamus?" Noah asked quietly. "We know Younger's been spending a lot of time at the pub lately. He says your brother has become obsessed with microbrews? He set up something in that studio behind Finn's Pub."

Owen nodded. "He's been talking about that since we started construction. He has a lot of plans for the place. I'm just glad he's focused on something positive. It's been a hell of a year for him." Especially the last few months.

Stephen might be the star of the Finn fold, and Owen the spoiled charmer, but Seamus was the good son. He spent the most time with their parents, taking care of them when they were ill, bringing the kids over every chance he got. He'd worked for their father when Shawn started slowing down and took over the pub from him when it was time to retire. Without fail Seamus always did what needed to be done, and he did it with love in his heart and a smile on his lips.

Despite bad luck in the romance department and the collection of children he was raising as a single parent, he was the true rock of the family. And that rock had been shaken. In one year he'd discovered Owen was gay and that his twin, Stephen, had been keeping his relationship with Tasha a secret since college. He'd almost lost his youngest son when that ass Burke brought Little Sean's mother back to sue for a custody she didn't want. As if that weren't enough, a few months ago they'd all found out their baby sister was sleeping with her college professor. The confrontation that followed not only showed them they were misinformed—she wasn't sleeping with one older man, but two—but the hits just kept on coming. Most of them having to do with their mother and her handling of Jen's romantic tangle.

It made Owen uncomfortable, knowing that the same woman who embraced his new status without hesitation and spent months obsessing over his wedding had given his sister such a hard time. It was so out of character. Their mother was the epitome of unconditional love for all of them. Until this happened. He didn't like to think of Jen having sex—ever—but Ellen Finn had been taking out her own issues, reliving her own mistakes through her only daughter. *Ellen* had slept with two brothers who were both in love with her and, in choosing one to marry, believed she'd created the rift between them. She'd been too ashamed of what people would say back then to keep them both, and she'd tried to put that shame on Jennifer, not understanding how different the situation was.

Shawn told Owen it was Sol's choices and selfishness that were to blame, and his choice to stay away. He'd convinced his wife to make things right with Jen after their confrontation nearly cost them their relationship. Owen was relieved as hell that they seemed to be good again. Better. Because he'd sure as hell had no idea how to fix it.

Seamus, however, had taken it harder than he had. He'd been absent more often than not at Finn Agains and family gatherings lately. Nearly as often as their cousin James. It had really screwed with the family dynamic. The kids still got to come, but everyone missed Seamus.

The wedding was helping. Seamus was throwing the small bachelor party tonight at the pub, and he'd promised he and the kids wouldn't miss the wedding or

Christmas morning. Which was good. It really wasn't the same without him around.

"We've lost him." Wyatt was snapping his fingers in front of Owen's face. "Worried about your brother, or mooning over Jeremy again? Because that would just be sad and I'd feel more like taking you to rehab than this party."

Owen narrowed his eyes. "Just wait, Wyatt. When it's your turn? Just wait."

"Man, you'll be eighty and looking for your teeth before that day comes. Noah might be the next one to drop, but not me. I'm single for life."

"I know that's what the women you sleep with keep telling you, Wyatt. But never give up." Rory sent him an innocent expression and Noah barked out a laugh.

"We're getting off topic."

"Did we have a topic?"

He took another drink of his beer and focused on Owen. "You *are* the topic. The groom and his wedding jitters."

He didn't have jitters. "Fuck off. Go bother Jeremy. He's a groom too."

"Jeremy is jitter free. I think you two would've gotten together a lot sooner if I was wrong about you

35

avoiding change."

"Good point," Wyatt tacked on, tapping his full lower lip thoughtfully. "But I totally get why Owen held off. I mean, this isn't like a move to a new apartment is it? It's a big step from ladies' man to LGBT poster boy."

"I guess. *If* you really believed you weren't gay," Rory said with a devilish smirk. "As for me I always knew Owen had it in him. I also know from experience that the straighter they think they are the harder they fall. But they have a hell of a lot of fun on the way down."

Wyatt punched his brother's arm. "We get it, okay? You're the all-seeing king of Gay Land and straight guys fall at your feet. Get another hobby already."

"But I'm so good at this one."

Noah met Wyatt's gaze and they spoke in unison. "We know, Rory."

It was hard not to laugh as Owen walked around them and headed to the kitchen for something to drink that wasn't beer.

Noah had a point. Owen liked things the way they were, so much that it took him forever to admit to himself that he wanted Jeremy. That his curiosity and jealousy and constant need to be near his best friend were all red flags that he might want more from their relationship.

He also wasn't much on talking things out. He liked his actions to speak for him instead. But finally getting around to saying he was gay made everyone happy and won him a fiancé in the process.

He might be slow, he defended himself silently, but when he made up his mind he went for it. He was as committed to Jeremy as he'd ever been to anyone or anything in his life.

Would marriage change them? Would the desperate need to rip each other's clothes off disappear? He doubted it. He'd dealt with all his fears about their relationship before he'd proposed, but he couldn't get rid of the knot in his stomach. Wedding jitters on steroids.

"Are you sure you don't want a beer?" Rory was leaning against the fridge. "It might make the day go faster."

Owen shook his head, reaching for the carafe of orange juice Jeremy kept on hand instead. "I'm good."

"You're not good, Owen. You're great," Rory corrected, his blue eyes dark. "You're marrying your best friend. A man so talented in the sack that he made you switch teams permanently. I'll be honest, I wouldn't mind knowing his secret."

Owen laughed. "You mean you've exaggerated your skills? Is there actually a man in the world you *can't* seduce?"

"I never exaggerate my skills. I don't have to. Let's just say Jeremy and I had a lot in common until recently, wanting someone who was off limits."

Owen's smile dimmed. "I didn't know you had limits." Or that he wanted one man in particular. "But you never know, Rory. Take me for example. Stranger things and all that."

Rory shrugged lazily, but it was clear the conversation made him tense. "Unfortunately my limit isn't even curious. He'll never bend that way and I'm not willing to put him in that position. Period."

"Sounds serious." Too serious for his carefree cousin. "Do you want him to? Bend?"

His cousin's voice was tinged with resignation. "Let's not go there. The point is you got the big prize. The one everyone wants but doesn't believe is real. You and Jeremy know everything about each other, the good, bad and embarrassing, and you still can't stand being out of each other's sight. Family, friendship, sex and romance—one man is that whole package for you. I kind of hate you right now, so stop fucking pouting about a day of separation or Noah will keep giving speeches. He's going through a phase at the moment where he thinks he knows everything and it's irritating as hell. I miss the good old days when he acted like Wyatt's dumbass double. Just hang out with us and pretend you're having fun, okay? It's easier."

"Speaking of speeches," Owen said, taken aback. "Anything *else* you need to get off your chest, Rory?"

His grin was rueful. "Sorry. Tis the season and all. I get a little maudlin around the holidays. We all do. Sol was the original Grinch. If you weren't getting married I'd be taking double-shifts like James and avoiding flashbacks and my empty apartment until my vacation days."

"James is working on Christmas Eve?"

"No," Rory assured him. "Younger would never let that happen."

Owen set down his juice and put his hand awkwardly on Rory's shoulder. "I'm glad you're all here."

"I almost believed you," Rory said, grinning.

"I am." He wasn't lying. They were distracting him and Rory had said exactly the right thing. He still didn't like Jeremy's decision to sleep somewhere else until the wedding, but he let himself relax and as soon as he did, he felt it.

"I'm getting married," he said quietly, causing Rory to laugh out loud.

"No shit. *And* claiming Christmas forever as your anniversary. Did you think of all the extra presents that would come your way? Is that why you changed the date? Some of us are spoiled, aren't we?"

Owen let his smile widen. "Some of us are. And some of us should bring non-bending friends to my wedding. Take it from me, nothing makes a man more curious than the right kind of visual stimulation." He didn't mention what kind of visual had stimulated *him*. It sure as hell wasn't a wedding.

Rory's expression was doubtful, but something flickered in his eyes. "We'll see."

***

"Come on, Brady," Owen urged, slightly buzzed and enjoying himself. "You remember that *going all in* speech right? The Great Rumming? Do it. Your smack-talking single brothers need to hear all that wisdom from the man himself."

Brady made an unmistakable gesture that had the small crowd of men at the bar roaring with laughter.

Owen snickered. "Is that any way for a best man to treat the groom before his wedding? Do I have to add a new Finn Club rule?"

He glanced at Stephen, remembering their mother's sadness that he wasn't going to be Owen's best man. But Stephen let her know he'd rather sit this one out. At this point the wedding had to be the most talked about event in the city if not the state, and his brother was a sitting senator who'd been on the right side of history before this year's Supreme Court ruling. Stephen didn't want the day to be about him and his political beliefs. He wanted it to be about his brother. By having it in a private home they'd denied most press access, but Owen agreed to let one in to avoid a riot and help his brother. She was a morning talk show host, young and seemingly in favor of the match and Stephen's voting record. He kept apologizing for that, but Owen couldn't care less. He wasn't hiding and he'd never been what anyone would call shy.

Anyway, as much as he loved his brother, Brady was the guy Owen wanted standing beside him, so it turned out perfectly. His mountain of a cousin had lived with Owen and Jeremy for a while, and he'd been the one who'd pushed him to talk about their future. To declare himself so the man he loved wouldn't wonder if he'd change his mind when he got bored with experimenting. The Marine gave good advice. Plus Badass kind of missed having him around the house.

"Good beer, Seamus," Solomon said gruffly beside them, looking out of place without his uniform. "Did the kids make the label for you?"

Seamus sent him a look. "Very funny. I'm still working out the kinks in my art department. Photoshop is a bitch. I do like the name for it though. Jeremy's Porter. It seemed right for the occasion."

"Owen's Porter would have been better," Owen mumbled, taking another drink. Jeremy was his after all.

"I like it," Rory said licking his lips as he took a drink. "Now we can all say we've tasted Jeremy. And he was dark and delicious."

Owen frowned when everyone groaned but still lifted their bottles to toast. "To Jeremy!"

"I told you there wouldn't be strippers." Wyatt's voice was loud in the sudden quiet and it started another round of laughter. "What? Bachelor parties in this family are sausage fests. Someone had to point it out."

Noah choked on his beer. "How about you stop pointing things out and practice that *shut-the-hell-up* we've been working on?"

Seamus slid Wyatt another bottle and shook his head. "This isn't that kind of pub, boys. We're a family place, it's Christmas, and a senator as well as the chief of police are sitting right next to you."

Solomon's expressionless features were completely at odds with the twinkle in his eye. "He's right, Wyatt. The place is too crowded as it is, since our cousin didn't see fit to close down the bar for his younger brother's only bachelor party."

Owen looked around. It wasn't *that* crowded. In fact, most of the tables were sparsely populated. All of them with people he knew. Owen narrowed his eyes. The women looked disturbingly familiar.

"I have kids to feed," Seamus defended. "I can't afford to close the bar every time something happens in a Finn's love life. Which lately? Is every other Tuesday. Owen understands it's just business."

Stephen chuckled. "Way to sell it, brother."

Owen frowned suspiciously at those words, glancing again at his men from Finn Construction and a few of James and Solomon's buddies from the precinct. And those women... He could swear they were actively ignoring him and trying not to smile. "What's going on here, Seamus? Who did you invite?" *Because I'm pretty sure I've slept with that brunette.*

Solomon stood and raised his bottle before Seamus could answer. "The city's most notorious bachelor—"

"Hey!"

Everyone looked at Rory. "Fine," Solomon growled in warning. "*One* of the city's most notorious bachelors is getting married."

Brady came to stand beside his older brother, grinning down at Owen. "Over the years, the star quarterback turned construction worker and business owner has made a lot of women happy—"

"Countless," Noah offered helpfully.

Brady dipped his head. "*Countless* women happy for a very little while." *Very little?* Several women at the tables chuckled or snapped pictures with their phones and Owen sighed, his suspicions confirmed. He'd dated them. And he was going to kill whoever invited them later. Brady continued, "After that excessive preparation, all he has to do now is make one man happy for the rest of his life. Let's hope his shamrock collection brings him luck, because he's going to need it."

Owen returned his earlier gesture, but Brady just winked and motioned to Stephen, who held his bottle aloft as well. "I say this as a brother and not a politician. Owen was always a pain in the ass," he started smoothly, causing snorts and guffaws. "He got away with murder and no matter what rule he broke or scrape he got into, he always ended up on top. Our mother's golden child."

"She did say I was special." Owen shrugged. "*You* had to run for public office to become the favorite." His smirk was teasing. If they were going to roast him, he could give as good as he got.

"True enough." Stephen pursed his lips over laughing blue eyes. "But despite his flaws, he did have great taste in friends. Having Natasha and Jeremy around the house almost made up for his less attractive traits."

"We all liked having Tasha around," Seamus said with a knowing grin, making his twin scowl in his direction.

"Yes, my *wife* has that effect. But we aren't talking about her." Stephen raised his voice again. "The only time any of us could stand Owen's company was when Jeremy was around. So I know I speak for all of us when we ask that he not screw it up. For everyone's sake."

"Here, here!" The crowd drank.

Owen bit his cheek to keep from smiling. Tasha had definitely loosened his brother up. "I'll do my best."

"One more." Seamus now. "I'm not exactly an authority on the subject of love, but working here I've seen my fair share of the search for it. And I have the bartender's curse of knowing it when I see it in other people. I see it in you Owen, when you look at Jeremy. I see it in him every time you're in the room." He looked into Owen's eyes. "You two have the real thing. All the happiness in the world, baby brother. I couldn't be prouder." He opened a bottle for himself and tipped it toward Owen. "To love and marriage."

The men at the bar joined him. "Love and marriage!"

Owen's throat was tight. "Thanks, Seamus. You were always my favorite."

Seamus and Stephen laughed together then glanced as one toward Solomon, who motioned to one of the tables. "Officer Wayne? We're ready to give Owen Finn the send-off his legendary bachelor days deserve."

A black man with heavy-lidded eyes and deep dimples nodded, getting to his feet. A friend of James, Owen thought, trying to remember where he'd met him before. Whoever he was, his knowing smile was alarming as he walked to the front door, glancing at Solomon once more before opening it with a flourish.

The band took that as their cue and began to play a

raunchy song as a line of firemen and policewomen poured into the pub and headed straight for the new dance floor. Much to Wyatt and Rory's delight, both men and women began to undress to the beat.

"My faith in you is restored." Wyatt gave his older brother a thumbs up.

"Wait, so all I have to do to get a stripping coed flash mob is marry a *guy*?" Noah raised his voice to be heard over the sudden din. "What if I married two of those women at the same time? Would that earn me a naked parade?"

"Not cool," Wyatt pointed at the costumes before rubbing his hands together. "You didn't have to hire fake firemen. The real thing is right here." They all watched as Wyatt tossed back his drink and joined the crowd on the dance floor, flinging his shirt over his head as the women who'd joined their party screamed their approval at his lean-muscled frame and shaggy dirty-blond hair.

"He took off his shirt again," Noah sighed. "I'm starting to hate that calendar."

Owen couldn't stop laughing. He leaned over the bar and gripped his brother's wrist. "This is insane, Seamus. Who came up with this?"

Stephen pressed in next to Owen and grinned. "Who

do you think?"

It was easy enough to guess. "*Tasha*? You let Tasha plan my bachelor party *and* Jeremy's? That's too much power for one woman to have. Especially that woman."

Seamus disagreed. "Are you willing to tell the bedridden senator's wife carrying my nieces and/or nephews that she can't have anything she wants? Because I'm not."

"I'm definitely not," Stephen spoke over the music, frowning as he looked down at his phone. "She said I'm not allowed home for another hour, but Jen's been sending me text updates and I have Trick on standby in case she needs anything."

Seamus frowned. "You should have invited him to the party, Stephen. Especially since Declan couldn't come."

"Shit." Stephen paled. "You're right."

"Relax, Stephen." Owen put his arm around Stephen's shoulders and squeezed. "He knows you're distracted. You can buy him a drink later, and before you know it you'll be holding two new Finns in your arms and Tasha will be causing more trouble than you can handle."

"I can't wait." If Owen hadn't been staring at him he

would have missed the words. Stephen was a mess. Since Tasha had been diagnosed with preeclampsia, he'd been doing everything in his power to keep her spirits up and her body in bed. Tasha was really going stir-crazy if this mob of strippers was any indication.

If she'd done this for him, what the hell was she doing for Jeremy?

"Owen! You're missing the show," Rory called, already grinding between two muscular men wearing little more than thongs and big yellow boots. From the surprised expressions on their faces, they'd been expecting women to be sliding bills into their pants. But neither one of them was moving away. They couldn't take their eyes off his attractive cousin.

Rory had clearly picked his next victims.

Owen waved him away with his free hand, gave Stephen's back a firm, comforting pat and excused himself. He needed a minute before he could go back in and be the smiling guest of honor they deserved.

He pulled out his own phone and his fingers were texting before he could stop himself.

A bar full of naked cops and firemen. Top that.

The response came less than thirty seconds later.

Are your cousins drunk again or is it the strippers?

How did you know there were strippers? What did she get you?

We're just talking here. Clothes on. And eating cakes shaped like my penis.

Owen snorted, moving toward the back door to the alley where he'd demanded Jeremy get on his knees. He'd done it for him again after Owen had proposed. Damn, he wished he were here now. *Your penis specifically?*

She made the mold years ago. I forgot but she kept it. Top that.

Can't top it, but I want to taste it. Bring it to me now.

Jeremy responded by sending a picture of Jen and Tanaka taking comically erotic bites of their penis cakes. *Hungry?*

Cake tease.

Owen sent him the picture he'd taken earlier of the beer Seamus made. *This is good but it doesn't taste as delicious as the real thing. I miss you.*

I'm a beer and a cake now? Miss you too. Enjoy the strippers.

As long as you don't.

I can't. Tasha sent them all to you so you couldn't complain.

A silver lining. *I'll call you when I get home.*

Owen slid his phone back in his jacket pocket and chafed his hands. He should be inside enjoying the show. What was wrong with him?

"Were you surprised? Your sister-in-law went all out."

Owen whirled in the alley and saw the tip of a cigarette burn red before it fell to the ground, snuffed out by his cousin. "Hey, James. I thought you quit."

"I did." The graveled voice was subdued. "I am. Just needed a break." He moved into the light, rubbing the back of his neck as he glanced back toward the pub. "I'm not big on crowds. Solomon swore this was a family thing. A few friends. He didn't mention the strippers until we got here."

You're not big on family gatherings either, Owen thought quietly. James was always taking extra shifts at the station on Finn Again nights and holidays. He was either the busiest police detective in the city, or he used his schedule to avoid socializing. "Rory says you don't have to work during the wedding. You'll be there?"

James looked up and Owen was startled for a second, the way he always was when he saw this particular Finn. He had the same hard expression and strong jaw as

51

Solomon. The same tall, lanky build. But his hair was so dark brown it was almost black, and his eyes were green instead of the usual Finn blue.

"Of course. And so will Elder. I'm taking care of that personally."

"You actually talked your dad into coming?"

James quirked his lips subtly in a smile that disappeared as quickly as it arrived. "Not yet. But I still have thirty-six hours or so. He'll be there. I won't let Shawn down again, though I can't promise anything more than his presence. He's made an art form out of being stubborn."

He remembered the engagement party. James and Solomon had both done their best to drag him to the pub, but Sol refused. It was a miracle the old man had made it to *any* of the family dinners, Owen knew, but that hadn't lasted long once Sol realized Shawn wasn't at death's door. Still, everything was out in the open now. No more secrets. Owen wasn't sure if that would help or make things worse. "Thank you."

"You shouldn't thank me. He's not much fun at parties." James shrugged. "What's your excuse?"

"What?"

"Why are you out here avoiding your bachelor bash?

This is a big night for you."

Owen smiled and leaned against the brick. "Yeah. She went all out, you're right about that." Now that he knew Tasha had been in charge of the planning, he had a good idea about who'd invited his ex-girlfriends to his party. Troublemaker. She was lucky she was so pregnant. "Everyone is great. But this is *not* the big night. Honestly, I wish it were over."

James narrowed his gaze. "That's a hell of a thing to say."

He held up his hand. "No, I mean I'm ready *now*. I want to be married *now*. I need it to be official so nothing can stop it and he can't change his mind."

A genuine smile cracked the unforgiving lines of his cousin's face. "He'll never change his mind, Owen. A blind man could see Porter's heart. The man wears it on his sleeve for you."

"I know." There was no way he would ever doubt it again. "I'm not changing my mind either. I don't think everyone believes *that* yet, but it's true."

"I believe it." James patted his pocket and scowled, flexing his fingers so he wouldn't reach for another cigarette. "You've changed since you two got together. Grown up."

"It only took thirty-six years," Owen said mockingly, wondering how James saw this big change when he was never around. "Since it *is* my party and I'm the guest of honor, can I ask you a question?"

His cousin stilled, already on alert. "I suppose."

"What's up with you? Why have you been playing the Finn family ghost? Most of the year, if we've seen you at all, it's for a few minutes at a time before you're gone again. Did we do something to piss you off?"

James flinched. "I'm just busy, Owen. I don't have the leisure of taking a night off every time the Finns want to get together."

Owen snorted. "Everyone works, James. But we make time. Family is—"

"The most important thing? I've heard that before and I know it better than most. But you're forgetting the Finns aren't my only family, Owen." James blew out a frustrated breath. "I'm sorry. Younger's been riding my ass about my absence for a while now. But I *am* working, and I *am* trying to spend time with both of my families. Just because he doesn't want to know Donna doesn't mean... It's not a big deal. I'm a jackass."

"No, I'm the jackass," Owen grimaced. "I know we go overboard with the Finn obligations. It isn't really fair to you and Solomon, is it? Hell, it wouldn't be fair to anyone who married into this mob." Though so far their significant others didn't have that much of a family to begin with.

He sometimes forgot that James and Solomon's mother, Donna, was still around. She'd given up her rights to them after a fight, but that didn't mean they didn't know about her or spend time with her now. Sol's other two wives had passed away, but even before then, his uncle had made it nearly impossible for anyone else to get their hooks into his sons. They were Finns. End of story.

He was a fucked up old man, and judging from his older sons and their tightly controlled personalities, he must have mellowed with age. None of the others were as grim as Solomon and James.

James growled and pulled out his lighter, clenching it in his fist like a talisman. "Don't apologize. You don't know what it means to Younger…to all of us to get the chance to reconnect with the rest of you. Just not really used to it. Your dad—You're lucky, Owen. Your side of the family, I mean. All I am is jealous."

"*Our* family. And James, don't sa—"

"It's true," he said in a low, dark voice. "We are

prime examples of that nature versus nurture shit, right? One side is all acceptance and unconditional love. The other..." His laugh was dark. "Let's just say if the shoe was on the other foot, things wouldn't be all sunshine and strippers."

"What do you mean?"

"I mean as Shawn's children you can do anything you want. Love anyone you want. Your brother married a dominatrix with paternal links to the IRA and now he's the most popular senator in the state."

Owen frowned at his words. "Technically she's a switch. And she's only half Irish. You left out black and Puerto Rican, not that it matters."

James held up two fingers. "Then your sister falls for two older bisexuals—one of them an ex-con and the other a Kelley. A hard pill to swallow for any family, but every Finn to a man deals and manages to accept them into the fold. Hell, *you* decide to get married in their house."

"Have you seen that house, James? I'd be crazy not to. And it wasn't as easy as you're making it sound. You know that."

But he was on a roll. "You also decided you were gay in your thirties and a little over a year later you're having the most celebrated wedding since the Prince kissed Kate. All this and your father still beams with pride at all of you. Your mother still showers you with affection. Everyone in the city is behind you."

Owen was bristling now. "And do you have a problem with any of that?" If he did, then he could take another double shift and stay the fuck away from his wedding.

"No, damn it, that's not what I'm saying." He swore under his breath. "This is why I don't like crowds, you know. Or Finn Agains. I'm better with criminals. I'd rather people I care about didn't realize how much like Elder I'm getting. I have his unique ability of always saying the wrong thing. I'm not judging, Owen. I'm *envious*. Not an attractive emotion, but there it is. You have a freedom I don't. I wish… I wish I could be like the rest of you."

Owen couldn't decide if he was pissed off or sympathetic. And he wasn't sure where it was coming from, but it was clear whatever James was going through, he was doing it alone. At least, without the Finn side of his family there to help him through it. "If we're playing this game, your brother Brady is lucky too." Owen took a step closer, watching his cousin warily.

"He found Ken and we're all good with it. Great with it. Rory's inside right now with two strippers who thought they were straight. And if they all moved in together tomorrow? We'd throw a party."

James snorted.

"We'd feel the same way if you found someone that made you happy, James. And you do have freedom. It's the freedom not to give a shit about what your father thinks. It works for your brothers. Why do you think it wouldn't work for you?"

He didn't answer and Owen swore in frustration. "You *are* being a jackass, James Finn. And if I hear you talking that shit at my wedding you and I will have words, detective or not. But you're still a part of this family. I know we're not the only ones in your life, but we're here if you need us. You just have to actually show up and ask."

James pinned him with a gaze so intense Owen wanted to step back. "You say that now," he said gruffly. "But you don't really know." He shook his head. "Do me a favor and forget I spewed all this bile at your bachelor party. Just remember that I truly am proud and happy as hell that you found what you wanted, grabbed on and didn't let go. I may not be acting like it tonight, but I hope you know how I feel."

"I know." *I love you too, asshole.* Owen tried to smile, putting his hand on a tense shoulder. "Why don't you come inside and have a drink with me? We can laugh at your brothers together."

"Not tonight." He backed away apologetically, still squeezing his lighter. "I'm not in the right place for it. I knew before I did I... I just wanted you to know I was here. Shit, I need to tell Hugo I'm bailing. But I'll bring Sol to the wedding. I promise."

"What the *hell*?" Owen muttered as James disappeared. The usually silent, more usually absent Finn had just dropped a lifetime's worth of frustration in the alley, but Owen had no idea what to do with it. And who was Hugo?

He hated this. People didn't usually tell him things. They told Jeremy things. They trusted and confided in his other half because *he* always knew what to say. Always had the right answers. Videogames and football? Owen was your man. Need a new building put up? Talk to Owen. Want to experiment with paddles and sadomasochism in the bedroom? Again, he should be first on your speed dial. But this? Owen was at a genuine loss.

He turned and went back inside the pub, determined to find Solomon and get a few answers. At the very least, it would distract him from missing Jeremy. And maybe they could bring James back from wherever he was heading. His cousin needed a Finn-tervention.

CHAPTER THREE

Brady Finn

1 day to Christmas Eve…

"I can't believe you ate Jeremy's penis cake."

Ken smiled, his long black hair spilling across the pillow as he looked up at Brady with hungry eyes. "Good morning. I was wondering when you'd find your way home."

Brady just stared until he laughed. "What? I was only trying to get in the familial spirit of things. Tasha was so pleased with herself for making Jeremy uncomfortable I couldn't resist. It even had filling. How's the groom holding up?"

Brady grimaced, pulling his t-shirt over his head. "As

well as can be expected considering. Still spoiled. I swear he'd be fine if no one told him he *wasn't allowed* to see Jeremy until the wedding. It took a lot of distraction and liquor to knock him out after the goodnight call to his fiancé. I left the boys to deal with his hangover, so we won't have to go back until tonight."

"We?"

Ken opened his arms as Brady crawled in naked beside him. He inhaled deeply and felt himself truly relax for the first time in hours. "God, you smell good. I missed you."

"I like hearing that." Hands caressed and massaged his back, soothing and arousing at the same time. "You said we," Ken reminded him softly.

"I have best man duties. We have to be there to make sure Owen gets to the wedding in one piece. I don't trust the boys alone. Not for something this important."

Noah, Wyatt and Rory were the perfect choices to distract Owen. It was the main reason Brady had enlisted them. They'd drive him so crazy he wouldn't be thinking about the big day until he was standing next to Jeremy saying his vows.

He'd had no idea James would help him with his

plan, however unintentionally. Owen spent hours last night—not enjoying the strippers Tasha had hired for him—but wondering what was wrong with Brady's brother. Had he been made by the mob? Was he sick and not telling anyone? Pregnant with an alien love child? What? Brady didn't have any answers, other than the obvious. Hell, he didn't even know there'd been a question.

"I'm a bad brother," he mumbled into Ken's neck, kissing him as his hand started to wander.

"Boy Scout, you couldn't be a bad anything," Ken assured him. Brady could feel his heartbeat race against his lips. "What happened? In between the beer and firemen I mean."

"Something's wrong with James."

"Any specifics?"

"I have no idea, but it doesn't sound good. And if Owen's drunken ramblings when I put him to bed have any merit, he's not the only one. Rory's unhappy too."

"That's harder to believe. Someone sent over a picture of Rory last night and he looked like he was having his usual amount of fun. And by that I mean too much with two men."

"I'm serious."

Ken wrapped one strong, slender leg over Brady's hip, squeezing seductively. "And you should have already known your brothers were having problems, because your Finn blood is magically delicious and links you psychically?"

"I should have known because we're brothers." He shivered at the way Ken was scraping his short nails along his skin. He was practically purring he loved it so much. "What do you think you're doing?"

Ken slid one hand between them in answer and did something that made Brady's breath catch in his throat. "I know you have a big...hero complex, but you can't solve all their problems right now. We have the wedding and Christmas to think about first. But we helped one Finn catch his bride. We could do it again if we put our heads together."

Brady couldn't help but smile. Ken always took the credit for that. They'd removed the last obstacles sure, but those two were like magnets. Eventually Stephen and Tasha would have come back together with or without Tanaka's hacking skills. Brady's fingers circled Ken's growing erection and tightened on hot, hard flesh. "Our heads? Is that what you're trying to put together?"

"Among other things."

Brady stroked him once. Teasing. "So you want to make Sol's single boys our next project? What if their problems have nothing to do with being single?"

Ken thrust himself impatiently into Brady's tight fist. Someone missed him. "Ken?"

"Yes," Ken gasped. "You know I love our projects. And we can solve any problems they have…but we can't leave Seamus out. He's the only single cousin you have left and he definitely needs help in the romance department. Oh God, do that again."

"You're impatient this morning," Brady growled, lowering his head to bite Ken's hard stomach teasingly before flipping him over on the bed and dragging him up to his knees. "Not that I'm complaining."

"There's my beast." Unmistakable satisfaction clung to Ken as he looked over his shoulder at Brady. "I was worried you might be too tired out after that all night stripper party to give me what I wanted."

Brady's smile was wicked. "Were there strippers? I didn't notice. And I could be comatose and it wouldn't matter if you were around." Brady lowered his body over Ken's for a kiss filled with biting lips and tangling tongues. His body reacted the way it always did to this man. Only this man.

He could hardly remember what his life was like before Kenneth Tanaka. Hardly believed he'd ever tried to resist him. His heart started beating the day he'd woken up in Ken's bed with a hangover from hell and no memory of the night before. He'd teased Owen for his codependence on Jeremy, but if someone told him he couldn't be with Ken? If someone tried to keep him away, even if *Ken* was that someone? Well, he already knew from experience he wouldn't be worth a damn without him.

Ken was groaning into his mouth, arching his hips in a not-so-subtle plea. Brady reached for the lube by the bedside and coated his erection, rubbing the excess between the cheeks of Ken's tight, tawny ass and slipping two fingers inside.

"What is it you want?" He wrapped long thick hair around his fist, tugging. "This?" The head of his cock pushed inside those tight clenching muscles and he made a raw sound of need. "What about this?"

Ken moaned. "*Yes*. All of it."

That primal feeling that overtook him every time they were together was back, filling Brady with the need to possess. "All of it," he snarled as he felt his lover's muscles tighten around his shaft when he was all the way in. "This is what I spent the night imagining. Waiting to come home to."

Ken's laugh was ragged and broken. "Did the firemen get you hot, baby?"

"You get me hot and you know it," Brady muttered, his jaw pulsing with restraint, his body focused on drawing this out. "Your mouth full of cock cake drove me insane. It reminded me of the last wedding we went to. Remember? You were on your knees, taking every inch of me down your throat."

"Oh God," Ken moaned when Brady's hands tightened in his hair. "It was just cake. I'd rather have you. Harder, Brady. *Please*."

Yes.

Brady heard the guttural sounds escaping his throat as he gave Ken exactly what he asked for. What they both needed every time they came together. *More.* They were perfectly matched in this, the way they were in everything. Better together. Stronger together.

More together.

He lost track of time, of everything but this—watching his cock disappear inside Ken's tight ass and feeling that bruising grip around his shaft. Listening to Ken's needy cries, the sensual sounds he never held back. They got Brady hot enough to combust. His skin was slick with sweat and his muscles ached with the effort to stay in control. He didn't want it to end. Not yet.

Ken took one hand off the bed and reached for his erection, but Brady was ready for that, forcing it back to the bed. "We both know you don't need help," he murmured hotly in Ken's ear. "Not when I'm fucking you."

"You're not fucking me. You're teasing me and I need to come, damn it." The plaintive admission tore at his control. Decimated it completely.

Jesus. Brady let go and the bed groaned with the force and speed of his next thrusts. Ken arched his back and let out a choked, "*Yes*" before pressing his head down onto the mattress and clawing at the sheets beneath him.

"Is this what you wanted?" His voice was thick with lust, all thoughts of control long gone. "Were you thinking about this when you knew I was in a room full of naked men without you?"

"Yes." Ken's throat was raw. "God yes."

"Did you imagine me bending you over a table and showing them how it's done? How much you can take? I know what an exhibitionist you are."

"*Yes.*"

Brady reveled in the feel of their bodies coming together, hard and fast, but he wanted more. He pulled out, making them both groan out loud, then turned Ken onto his back and lifted his legs until his knees were pressed into his shoulders. One forceful thrust had him deep inside again and he stayed like that for a few gasping moments, trying to see Ken through the haze of need blinding him.

"Rope Master Tanaka thinks a few college boys who pump iron on the weekends can hold a candle to him? I don't believe it." He pulled back and thrust deep again, making them both shudder. "That's not my super hacker." *Thrust.* "That's not my—*Fuck.*"

Ken squeezed his internal muscles and lifted his hips for the next thrust, making the fit so tight and deep there were dark spots behind Brady's eyes. "Stop talking, Brady."

"Yes, Master." Brady saw Ken's blown out pupils and knew he was close. He picked up the rhythm that would push them both over, holding him down with the weight of his big body so he couldn't do anything but take it.

"Brady…God, baby. *Yes!*" Ken's orgasm hit them like a wave breaking hard on the rocks. He was shaking, his come pumping out onto his smooth chest.

"*Ken.*" Brady jerked and shivered hard as his orgasm seized him and wouldn't let go. *Love you*, he thought, filling Ken with his release. *Love you…*

***

It was late afternoon when Brady padded out of the bathroom in nothing but a towel, searching for Ken and—when his stomach grumbled loudly—something to eat. They'd spent most of the morning wearing each other out, Ken more insatiable than usual. Brady passed out around noon and when he opened his eyes again, he knew he was alone in the bed.

He poured a cup of eggnog and grabbed a handful of mixed nuts from the bowl on the counter, looking around the living room. They'd decorated a few weeks ago, after Brady told Ken about holidays with Sol. Elder wasn't that big on…well anything really, but he seemed to have an extra dose of hate for this holiday season. Brady used to think it was because he'd been a cop for so many years. Christmas wasn't all carols and tidings of joy. There was generally an uptick in crime as well.

Whatever the case he and his brothers rarely had a reason to look forward to December.

Ken hadn't celebrated the holidays since he'd lived with Patricia and her sons, so they decided to go all out. Now the classy loft looked like the damn North Pole and smelled like a pine tree...and Brady loved it. He also loved that Ken had done this for him. The memory of them standing naked in the living room stringing lights and trying to come up with new lyrics to their favorite childhood carols would stay with him forever.

Ken's phone and keys were on the coffee table and his shoes were by the door, which meant he was still in the building, just not the loft. What was he up to?

Not bothering to dress, Brady opened the front door and stepped across the hall to the newly renovated office. A few months ago Ken had trashed the large room filled with computers and hardware he'd used to create and improve anti-hacking software for the government. As a freelancer, of course. Ken liked being his own boss. And he wasn't a stickler for rules or *Keep Out* signs.

Clad in a pair of boxer briefs, Ken was typing furiously on his keyboard, his hair tied back in a sloppy bun and his focus absolute. Or so Brady thought.

"You're finally awake. I thought I broke you."

He walked in and grabbed a chair, setting it beside Ken's. "I'm a fast healer. What's up? Already starting the Finn Project?"

Ken's lips twitched. "That's happening in another window and already looks promising. I'm multi-tasking. This," He nodded at the screen as a numeric message popped up. "This is your Christmas present. One of them."

Now he was intrigued. "Feel like giving it to me early?"

"Hang on. I just have to… There." He spun his chair toward Brady and took the cup, setting it on the desk beside his monitor and holding on to both his hands. "I think we did it. With a little help from Trick."

Brady tensed, completely alert now. He knew what Ken was talking about. "Which one?"

"Your favorite. He's alive, in custody and singing like a bird as we speak. They aren't taking any chances this time. He says he can connect the others to everything. Terry's disappearance. Cal's death. Vargas. I'm verifying some of his information for the authorities now. Including an offshore account used specifically for their more nefarious purchases."

They had Pony Boy. That was the name Brady had given to the youngest member of the Slaver's Club—a group of mega-rich untouchables that Brady and Ken had been chasing for months now. Ever since they'd teamed up to find Terry Wahl.

"I can't believe it." Brady shook his head, his fingers tightening on Ken's in reaction. "This is—"

"This is one hell of a domino, Brady." Ken's eyes were molten. "If he falls…"

"He will. I know he will. And by this time next year it'll be over. It was about time for the good guys to take home a win." Brady frowned. "He's already in custody? When did you find out this was going down?"

"A few days ago."

"And you didn't tell me because…?"

Ken tugged his hands away. "It was a Christmas present. I wanted to wait, to be sure, so I could tell you it was almost over and we could move on without this obsession between us."

Brady's eyes narrowed. His lover had pushed him away before when it looked like there was no winning this fight. Was he worried about the backlash that might come if they didn't do everything right? Worried about Brady's safety again? "This is a good thing, Ken. This is

73

fucking-a-fantastic. It means Patricia and Terry won't have to be in hiding forever. It means we don't have to be on high alert and hire people to watch our family day and night. We can relax and focus on better days."

He must have said something right, because one minute he was getting knots in his stomach, and the next Ken was climbing into his lap and savaging his mouth. Brady moaned and wrapped his arms around him. He wasn't sure what he'd said, but he didn't care anymore.

Ken pulled back, panting. "Our family doesn't get to give you a bachelor party."

Brady flinched. "What?"

"When I ask you to marry me," Ken began, rocking his hips seductively against Brady. "And you say yes? Our plans won't include separate bachelor parties and big receptions. We don't have to be that traditional. Right?"

"Right," Brady murmured absently, then stared at Ken, startled. "When you ask me to marry you?"

"And you say yes."

His throat felt tight. "So, this is a plan you have? You've thought about it a lot?"

"To be honest, the ban on strippers just happened last night." Ken shook his head. "I know, it's unexpected.

I'm in clubs where people walk around naked most of the time when I do demos. Naked is my favorite clothing trend next to rope. But," He shrugged. "Those fireman bugged me. I wanted to drive down there, tie you up and drag you home."

When I ask you to marry me. "Interesting."

"Isn't it?"

Brady scowled. Was he trying to be cute? "Did you have a timeline in mind for this proposal?"

Ken licked his lower lip, distracting him. "Well, it won't be Christmas. Your cousin made sure of that."

Fucking Owen. Brady lifted Ken enough to pull off his towel before pressing him down against his uncovered erection. "Makes sense. So, New Year's then?"

Ken hummed thoughtfully, rubbing and rocking until Brady swore under his breath. "Ken?"

"I'm thinking. We're still tying up a few loose ends on our last project, and we do have those single Finns to take care of."

Was he serious? "So your plan is to wait until every problem is solved and every single Finn hooks up before popping the question? Even Younger and James?"

"And Seamus. It would be good incentive. And you'd

have plenty of time to work on that positive response I'm expecting." Ken lowered his head to Brady's neck, scraping his teeth along the tense tendons. Was he smiling?

"Is this your sadistic side popping out? Another way to tie me up in knots?"

"Definitely."

He wasn't denying it. Brady picked him up, getting to his feet with ease. "Are you done here?"

"It's going to take a half an hour for the—"

"So yes."

Brady didn't let Ken catch his eye as he carried him back to the loft and into the brightly decorated living room. He knew he was surprised when Brady dropped him on the couch and stepped away. Knew he'd been expecting him to head straight for the bedroom for round four.

But there were other things on his mind.

When I ask you to marry me...

Naked and still fully aroused, he walked over to the Christmas tree and bent down to find the package he'd wrapped last week. The one he'd hidden underneath all the rectangular clothing boxes that Ken had teased were, "Just black t-shirts, because that's all you wear."

So many thoughts were swirling in his head when he picked it up. How he'd almost lost it when Ken pushed him away for his own good. How wrong he'd been about the kind of person the wealthy and unapologetically kinky Master Tanaka was, and what he wanted from a man. About how many times he'd been thankful that he was only the best man, because Finn weddings were insane.

"Not that I don't like the view, Marine, but you're not supposed to be shaking the presents. That's our rule." Ken sounded hesitant. Curious.

Brady stood and moved to the couch, pulling Ken easily onto his large lap as soon as he sat down and handing him the small box. "Here."

"But Brady—"

"You gave *me* an early Christmas present," he insisted, noticing how dry his mouth was and how loudly his heart was thrumming in his ears. "It's only fair."

He watched Ken in silence as he carefully undid the wrapping paper. When he opened the box, they both stared at the contents in silence. It was a ring. A wide titanium band delicately engraved with an image of a koi fish swimming around a dragon. Brady had taken a picture of Ken's back tattoo a few months ago for the jeweler. It seemed like a great idea at the time. The perfect gift for the man who had everything. A symbol to show him how serious Brady was about their relationship, in a way Ken couldn't help but understand.

When he'd picked it up he'd had second thoughts because, well, it looked like a wedding ring, and he wasn't sure Ken would go for that yet. It wasn't something Brady let himself hope for back when he was serving in the military. In his heart, he'd never believed someone would want him enough to make that kind of commitment. He'd gone back and forth about it until he'd finally wrapped it and put it under the tree so he wouldn't be tempted to take the damn thing back to the store.

Ken wasn't moving. Wasn't looking away from the ring or making a sound. It made Brady nervous. "It's— do you see the design? You told me that to you it meant becoming more than you were yesterday. Moving forward."

Ken reached for the ring and placed it on the tip of his forefinger, turning it so it glinted in the light. Brady couldn't stand the silence. "That's how I feel. With you, I'm more than I was. The nightmares are rare now. I'm not living in limbo or beating myself up about the past. I have my moments and I know I'm not perfect, but I'm happy. I wake up and you're there and…"

Silence. Shit had he gone too far? "I know it's early days and I wasn't sure—it doesn't have to mean—"

Ken gripped his face and kissed him. It was a soft kiss. Tender. It made Brady breathless. "So that's a yes?" he demanded, pinning Brady with his bright golden gaze.

"I thought you wanted to wait."

Ken made a sound of impatience. "Will you marry me, Brady Finn? I need to hear you say the word."

"Yes." Brady's smile was impossible to conceal. *He liked the ring.* "After we tie up our loose ends and single Finns."

Ken maneuvered him onto his back on the couch and straddled Brady's calves. "I wasn't married to that timeline."

Married. Jesus. Brady bit his lip when Ken lowered his head and planted an open-mouthed kiss on his cock. "It'll be an incentive. Your words."

"You think I need it?" Before he could answer Ken was taking all of him down his throat and moaning against his sensitive flesh.

"Fuck." Brady gripped the back of Ken's head and

pumped his hips up off the couch. "God, that's the sexiest damn…" His words trailed off as he raised his head to watch. If he was trying to suck him into submission it was working.

What Tanaka did with his mouth and the muscles in his throat was unfair. It made Brady want to beg. He'd do anything. Anything Ken wanted as long as he didn't stop. When he paused to lick Brady's shaft lightly he dug his fingers into Ken's scalp and threw one calf over his shoulder, trapping him. "Don't tease," he rasped. "I need you."

Ken instantly relaxed his throat and let Brady take the lead, groaning in pleasure as if he couldn't get enough. *The son of a bitch wants to marry me*, Brady couldn't help the amazement he felt at that thought.

When wet fingers slid inside Brady's ass, stretching him and pushing against his prostate he let out a strangled cry. "Don't stop." *Don't ever stop.*

One more thrust and he was shouting Ken's name and shuddering with the power of his release. He felt soft lips kiss his damp tip, his stomach and then his chest, and he loosened his hold on Ken's head long enough to wrap him in his arms as he draped himself across Brady's quaking body.

After his heart rate returned to normal and he could breathe again, Ken wriggled in his arms and he smiled. "I'm glad you liked that present, because the only other thing I got you was rope."

Ken laughed softly. "I have a lot of rope, Brady."

"And I have a lot of black shirts. We'll be more creative next year."

Ken lifted his head, his expression difficult to read. "Every year from now on. I'm part of your family now."

"Yes."

"You agreed to marry me."

Brady smiled. "Yes."

"With you, I'm more than I was."

God, this man had his heart. He nodded, for a minute too choked up to speak.

"But I can't come with you to Owen's tonight."

Brady frowned at the sudden change in topic. "Why the hell not?"

"I'm Team Jeremy." Ken shrugged helplessly. "It's not a very big team. He's an adopted Finn with no extended family of his own, so we have that in common. Plus he asked if I'd protect him from Little Finn and Tasha. Apparently they know exactly how to manipulate him and he's too distracted to resist."

Love and pride swelled inside him. Ken Tanaka was a good man. His man. "You should add Trick to the team," he offered helpfully. "He didn't come to either bachelor party and I'm sure Jen would appreciate the gesture."

Ken kissed his chin. "Good idea. And since I'll be there anyway, maybe Stephen can give me a few hints about what Seamus might be looking for in a love match."

"So it begins," Brady said, laughing. "Let's start with someone who isn't a pregnant damsel in distress, and go from there. Seamus deserves to be taken care of for once. And adventure. He needs a little adventure in his life." The kind this man gave him every day.

Ken's grin was the definition of trouble. "I think I have an idea."

CHAPTER FOUR

Trick

Trick had just gotten the strangest phone call from Tanaka. He smiled as he walked down the second floor hallway toward the staircase. Team Jeremy, huh? As long as he wasn't forced to eat the cream-filled penis cake Jen told him about, he was up for anything.

He supposed that meant he was officially a member of the club now. Maybe they'd make more t-shirts, because the name Finn wasn't seen enough in this town. Finn's pub. Finn Construction. Billboards that read, "Vote for Senator Finn." If he hadn't fallen in love with one and grown up with another, it would probably be irritating.

It was still, on occasion, irritating.

He chuckled and picked up his pace. Jen was Team Jeremy too. She already had an overnight bag packed for the pre-wedding slumber party at Stephen's. There'd been room for everyone to come here, but Stephen wanted his wife to stay in her own bed as long as possible. They were all doing their part to include Jeremy's closest friend and his *best woman*—as Tasha love being called—in every aspect of the planning. And she was definitely enjoying herself. Tanaka had told him about the pub full of exotic dancers she'd sent for Owen.

He was glad Declan had decided to stay home to oversee the workmen. But he always had something to oversee lately, and *of course* he was having something built specifically for the occasion. The good professor had flown in a damn chocolatier and a wedding designer. Not a planner. A *designer*. Which was another word for way too expensive for Trick to think about.

He'd tried to tell him Owen had only agreed to get married here because he had a media wall that took up half the giant living room—but once Declan started there was no stopping him. He'd spoken to Jeremy and Ellen Finn, Jen's mother, about his ideas, and a wedding monster was created that someone was eventually going to have to slay or Trick's happy family might never get their home back.

At least she was talking to Declan now. Nothing soothed a mother's heart like a professional wedding designer. Mrs. Finn still couldn't look Trick in the eye. But then, even if he weren't the other slice of bread in the Little Finn sandwich, he wouldn't be a mother's dream come true. An ex-con with tatted sleeves and a seedy job that was anything but nine-to-five. Trick Dunham might be old friends with Stephen, and he might have been a good choice to watch out for her daughter, but he wasn't husband material.

Professor Kelley was.

He could let himself get hung up on it, but there was no point in denying the truth. Hell, even Declan had taken it for granted that he was the better option—financially speaking—and he'd been right. They'd talked about it more than once, though never with Jen. Jennifer Finn was a beautiful, smart and independent woman who'd been overprotected by her brothers and would no doubt kick both their asses if she found out her men were secretly conspiring to make sure she was always taken care of. But there was no way it wasn't going to happen. They had to take care of her. Needed to protect her. She was too precious to both of them, and their instincts when it came to her couldn't be denied. Since Declan had more money than he would ever be able to spend, the problem was easy to solve. Jen would take his name and the multiple bank accounts and real estate that came with it. End of story.

It didn't bug him. It *shouldn't* bug him. Trick knew those two were crazy about him. Just as wild for him as they were for each other. He wouldn't have brought them all together if he hadn't been sure of it from the start. Twisted as it probably sounded to the outside world, the three of them fit. Trick had never felt so wholly satisfied. Not even when he and Declan were first together. Jen was always the missing piece. He'd realized it when following her stopped being a job and became his obsession. And even then he'd been aware that she wasn't his alone. She was meant to be Declan's too. The fiery, strong-willed redhead who loved seeing her two men together nearly as much as she loved joining them was their match in every way. She filled Declan's lonely life with love and gave Trick his first real home.

And after the New Year she'd be Declan's wife. The plan was already in motion. Trick would handle any uneasy twinges that cropped up on his part, because the only other option was losing what they had together, and that was unacceptable.

His steps slowed when he saw Declan standing on the landing looking down at the floor below. Trick knew what he was seeing. Lines of florists and caterers and cleaners. The queen bee planner and her hive doing their last minute checks and preparations for tomorrow. They'd been buzzing around all day, which was why Trick had spent most of it upstairs playing some childish gem game he'd found on Jen's tablet. That shit was addictive.

He bit his lip, studying Declan's backside and feeling his cock stir in his jeans. He'd always been an irresistible piece of ass. Brilliant, big in all the right places and sexually aggressive in the best way. He still remembered his initial reaction to Declan Kelley. How he'd fantasized about taking off those glasses and giving the buff bookworm a lesson in passion to pay him back for his tutoring sessions. He thought he'd be the one in control. That he'd be doing the seducing.

Trick had never been happier to be wrong.

He moved silently until he was standing right behind his lover. Declan was too lost in thought to notice he was no longer alone. He didn't like not being noticed and had to do something about it immediately.

Trick had one hand covering his mouth and the other cupping his dick and squeezing before he could make a sound. "Hey, Professor Hot Lips," he whispered, scraping his teeth over Declan's earlobe. "How's it hanging?"

The *it* in question was in his hand and getting harder with each passing second. Declan lifted his hands to cover Trick's on his mouth, but didn't struggle. "This brings back memories for me, Kelley. Frustrating memories of playing the bad boy, stringing our girl along with all her kinkiest fantasies until you finally gave in and let us all get what we wanted."

Declan's growl vibrated against his palm and Trick laughed. "I know you were jealous. But it was your own fault for trying to resist my plan."

Trick was surprised when Declan jerked out of his grip and leaned against the wall. He'd been turned on by Trick's touch, but something was definitely bothering him. "What's wrong? Do you need me to take out the wedding designer? Because I can and I will. Say the word and she and her entourage of ice artisans and pastry patsies will disappear like that." He snapped his fingers.

Declan's frown darkened. "Okay, not the problem. Care to clue me in, Professor?"

"Jennifer."

Trick moved closer, worry instantly gnawing at him. "What about her?"

"She said no."

Trick leaned heavily against the wall, unable to conceal his surprise. "You did it today?" *Without me?* "You actually asked her the day before her brother's wedding? Been sniffing one too many orange blossoms, Professor?"

Declan shrugged and pushed up his glasses, the confusion and embarrassment in his expressive gray eyes doing nothing to dim his good looks. She'd turned *him* down? Had Little Finn gone off her meds? It didn't make any sense.

"It slipped out. We were talking about last minute errands for the wedding and she mentioned being relieved that she'd been spared from marrying the wrong man."

"Let me guess," Trick said wryly. "You asked if she'd have a problem marrying the right one?"

Declan looked irritated. "Something like that. She laughed until she realized I wasn't joking. When I explained that you and I had discussed the benefits, that I'd gotten her father's approval… She didn't react well."

Trick was no longer questioning Jen's sanity. He was questioning Declan's. "Hell, man. You have all those degrees and I keep trying to give you the benefit of the doubt, but you're making it hard." He pinched the bridge of his nose. "I can't imagine a less romantic way to propose, unless you brought out a list of pros and cons. Tell me you didn't make a list. I'm begging you."

"I didn't get the chance," he answered, still brooding. "She told me she needed some space to think. And now she'll be spending the night with her sister-in-law, working herself up into never speaking to me again."

"I won't give her the chance," Trick assured him. "I've been invited to join them."

"You have?" Declan didn't look too happy about that. "So you're both leaving me?"

"You just want me to stay and help move those chairs around," Trick teased.

Declan started to walk away but Trick pushed him back against the wall, using his body to hold him where he wanted him. "Hey, it's only for the night. But I'll give you something to think about while we're gone."

Declan melted into the kiss, moaning as Trick's

tongue fought a sensual battle with his, tilting his head and offering everything. A question kept swimming around his desire drenched brain, refusing to disappear. "Did she use those words? Space to think?" Trick asked when he lifted his head to drag in some much-needed oxygen.

"What?" It was gratifying to see him so dazed.

"Is that exactly what she said?"

At Declan's nod, Trick smiled. "Follow me, Professor. We can fix this."

His first instinct was to pull Declan to the floor and distract him. It was his second and third instinct too. It always was. He could spend a lifetime enjoying Declan's body. But then his deep-thinking lover would spend the rest of the night angsting himself to death over what he should have said. Jen would act tough, but she wouldn't be much better.

Relationships were a lot of fucking work.

She was exactly where he knew she would be. Downstairs in the library, curled up in a chair and staring at Declan's art collection. He remembered when he told her about those paintings. That they were all of her, in one way or another. That he and Declan had always been waiting for her. Was she thinking about that now? Or wondering if they could still be together after she'd rejected Declan's offer?

"Hiding from the wedding chaos?" Trick asked lightly, his grip bruising on Declan's wrist as he dragged him inside and locked the door behind them.

Jen jumped and pushed back her mane of fiery hair, biting her lip. "I guess. I was just thinking about heading toward Tasha's."

Trick strode over to her and pulled her to her feet. "You're not dressed."

She looked down at herself with a frown. She was in yoga pants and a festive green Christmas shirt that said, *Just Say Ho*. "Yes I am. I'm only goi—"

He kissed her and she gasped into his mouth. One instant of surprise and then her stiff muscles were melting and her arms were lifting to wrap around his neck. Neither one of them could resist him. He used that to full advantage, pulling off her shirt and pushing her stretchy black pants down her legs. "Oops," he said wickedly. "I meant, you won't be dressed for a while."

"Do you know how many strange people are in this house right now?" She moaned when he dropped to his knees and bit the inside of her thigh as she stepped out of her pants entirely. "Trick…"

"Trick," Declan echoed, though his voice had an edge that told him he wasn't unaffected by his actions. "Maybe this isn't the best time."

He stood and palmed Jen's braless breasts, pinching her nipples roughly and making her back arch in reaction. "Because she said no to that sad proposal?" Jen jerked under his hands. "If you think that'll stop me, you're insane."

"He told you?" Jen's blue eyes went wide.

"Of course he told me. Clearly the man has issues with romantic proposals, but if he were perfect he'd be boring. And he has other qualities we both enjoy, so I guess we'll have to forgive him and fuck instead."

Her fair skin flushed and she glanced at Declan. "I'm not sure he'd be okay with that."

Trick tried not to smirk and failed miserably. "Declan? Take off your clothes and get the lube from your desk. She's not sure you're okay with having some quality Jen time before we're inundated with wedding guests and we have to monitor our behavior."

Declan's expression darkened dangerously and he started to unbutton his shirt in silence. Jen licked her lips, watching him. "He's upset."

"He's turned on. *I'm* upset," Trick murmured,

lowering his head to lick one hard, ripe nipple. "No one's asked me to take my clothes off yet."

Her hands immediately reached for the button of his jeans. "That's more like it."

He got lost in her taste, his mouth full of lush flesh, his fingers slipping through the wet heat between her thighs. She was just as turned on as he was. When Declan pressed himself against his back Trick groaned, hating the restraint that had him saying, "Not this time. On the floor, Declan. She'll be the one in control."

"She always is." He heard Declan's soft complaint and chuckled against Jen's skin.

He straightened and looked into her eyes. They were dilated, but he could still see a trace of uncertainty. "It's okay, I promise. Show him how much you love him, baby." He knew she did. Whatever reasons she had for turning him down didn't change what the three of them had together. When she didn't move he lowered his hands to the only clothing she had left—her lace underwear—and ripped it down the center. Her lips parted and he knew she was theirs. "Take these off and show him."

Jen got rid of the tattered panties and straddled Declan's thighs. Trick could see the big body beneath her trembling with restraint. The professor was used to being in charge. Being on top. His hands were clenched into fists and Trick sympathized, knowing how impossible it was not to touch her. Not to lose control around their wildly passionate woman.

He kicked off his boots and finished undressing swiftly, kneeling behind her and hissing out a rough breath when his erection brushed against her heavenly ass. "Do you remember that first night? In this room, watching us? I want to watch now, Jen. Touch him for me. Take him."

Declan's growl made her shiver, but she wrapped her fingers around his thick erection and lowered herself slowly onto him. They moaned in unison. "Declan," she gasped.

He didn't speak but Trick could see the fire in his eyes. "That's it," he whispered in Jen's ear. "He's holding back, but he needs you. Give him what he needs."

She put her hands on Declan's broad chest and started to move. They were beautiful together. So beautiful Trick couldn't look away. He watched Declan's hands, unable to remain still, grip her hips as he helped her set a powerful rhythm that had them both shuddering.

"So good, Jen."

"*God*, Declan."

Trick kissed her shoulder and pressed his erection into her back, his arm slipping around her waist. "I don't know how you do it, Jen. Just watch. I'm more of an action man myself. Greedy."

"Trick, please," she moaned, turning her head and kissing him. "I want you both."

He met Declan's stormy eyes and saw the approval. *Thank-fucking-God.* Trick grasped the bottle beside them and pressed Jen forward. "Kiss him. Kiss Declan while I get you ready for me."

Jen collapsed, kissing Declan almost angrily, biting his lower lip until he snarled and took control. *That's right, bad girl*, Trick thought in a lust-induced haze. *That's how we work out our problems in this house.*

He slipped one lubed finger between her cheeks and moaned when her ass tightened around it. He could feel every thrust of Declan's cock, the way her body reacted to their dual invasion, and he knew she didn't want him to go slow. He added a second finger and thrust deep.

"More," she cried out raggedly. "God, that's so good."

Declan was growling like a predator. He cupped Jen's ass and spread it for Trick, impatience in every rough movement. "I fucking love teamwork," Trick groaned with that first thrust, his body shaking at the tight squeeze. His hands tangled with Declan's on her hips and they all fell together. Lost. Then there were no more words, no misunderstandings, just garbled cries of need and the raw sounds of sex.

Trick closed his eyes and let it consume him. His desire for the two of them grew stronger every day they were together, but it didn't scare him. It made him as insatiable as Declan. As hungry as Jen. This was how he wanted to live and die. Feeling this. Knowing they were his.

"Fuck, she feels good, doesn't she, Professor. Isn't this better than brooding in separate corners?"

"Jen," Declan moaned. "So tight."

"Please don't stop," she gasped.

"Never, baby."

"Never say never." Trick wasn't going to last. He started a new rhythm meant to drive all of them up to the edge of the cliff and over.

"*Trick.*" Jen cried out and Declan swore beneath them, finding his release as Trick's thrusts jarred his body. Then Jen joined him with their names on her lips and Trick followed less than a raspy groan later. He couldn't think of anything clever to say, couldn't do anything but survive his body exploding apart and slamming back together.

Afterward they all collapsed on the library rug, Jen between them with her hands curled and trembling on their chests. "Where the hell did *that* come from?" she breathed drunkenly.

"Weddings make me horny?" Trick offered in a lazy tone, enjoying the sound of Declan's laughter.

"Weddings make you run for the hills as a rule," Declan responded.

"Not anymore. And it's all Jen's fault."

"How is it my fault?"

"It's always sex, sex, wedding, sex with these Finns. It's a wonder they have time to stop for food breaks or paying the bills."

Jen huffed out a laugh. "Owen and Jeremy are managing to resist the urge."

Trick snorted. "I doubt it. It was a shitty plan in the first place, but who is actually enforcing it? I'm having a hard time believing those two didn't find a way to sneak into each other's pants last night. They're worse than we are."

"Oh, I think we could win that competition if we tried," Declan said, his satisfied tone making Trick's dick stir again.

Jen laughed at them both and whacked Trick playfully. "They didn't sneak anywhere. Tasha made sure of it. And you're the bad influence, Tristan Dunham. There I was, having a good pout and you walked right in, ripped off my clothes and had your way with the two of us. Shameful." She bit her lip. "I love you for that. Both of you. I really hate fighting."

Declan pushed himself onto his elbow and Trick saw the vulnerability in his eyes. "We love you too, Jen. I…" He shook his head. "I don't want to fight with you. I apologize for upsetting you and the way I asked you. But not for asking. I can't be sorry for wanting that with you."

Jen lifted her hand to caress his shadowed jawline while Trick stroked her hip tenderly. "It was a surprise, that's all. Especially knowing you'd been discussing it without me. For future reference, that's another one of those conversations I should be in the room for."

"Agreed," Trick said immediately. "The next time Declan works up the nerve to ask you—in say, a week or so—we'll talk about it together over dinner. Or in bed when you're tied up and can't get away."

She shook her head and pushed herself up into a sitting position, covering her breasts. "We don't need to talk about it over dinner. I don't want to get married. Not now."

"Oh." Trick felt the same pain he could hear in Declan's simple word.

Jen sighed. "It's not because of either of you. Not directly. I was engaged for years, you know that."

"To the wrong man," Trick couldn't help but point out.

"The entirely wrong man," she agreed instantly. "I picked out invitations and auditioned bands and I didn't look up long enough to notice how wrong he was for me. Helping out for Owen and Jeremy has been fun, but it also brought up a lot of memories. Made me think about my future. Our future."

Shit. Conversations that started like this rarely ended well. "And you decided we were perfect and we all lived happily ever after in bed?"

She grinned down at him, lowering her arms as her shoulders relaxed. "And now I have two men, both entirely right for me. Both necessary for my happiness."

"But you don't want to marry us?" Declan asked quietly.

Jen turned into Declan's neck and nuzzled. "I do. That's the problem. I honestly can't imagine only marrying one of you, but I'm not an idiot. I know I can't marry you both. Not legally. Owen and Jeremy's wedding is important. Because they love each other. Because within my lifetime it wasn't legal. Because Jeremy belongs to my family and we should have that down on paper somewhere. But for us? It's only paper, Professor. And you know better than most that in other cultures we wouldn't need it to make a true and lasting commitment to each other. We've already done that. We belong to each other, in every way that counts. What we have is what matters."

"She's clever," Trick said to Declan with a smile. "And using your own class notes against you too. I warned you Finns were stubborn."

But Declan was still frowning. "What about children? Later, of course," he added hastily. "I know you still have your graduate studies."

Her smile was a siren's call. "What about them? I'm a healthy baby-making machine, according to my doctor. As soon as I stop taking the pill, of course. Tasha made me go just in case." She licked her lips and looked at both of them in turn. "*When* we have children in the not too distant future, I hope they're as smart as both of you, and a little less trouble than I was. Smart enough not to care whether or not their parents have a piece of paper that says they're married."

Declan had been talking about legalities and inheritance and she knew it, but she'd turned the tables on them. Her answer floored them both. "So, you wouldn't be opposed to having kids sooner rather than later?" Declan's face flushed, his eyes darkening with desire at the prospect.

Trick felt her hand cover his where it stilled on her hip. "Definitely not. This house is way too big for the three of us. Babies and pets are the obvious answer. We can get me that dog anytime, by the way."

"If there were twenty of us and ten dogs, it would still be too big." Trick hid his shaky smile against her shoulder.

Jen made a face. "Twenty is a hard limit. But maybe three or four little Dunham-Kelleys and a pair of Boxers would be nice."

"Dunham-Kelley?"

"If you don't *both* agree on that they'll be Finns," she

102

informed them smugly. "And you know I have no problem with—"

Trick pulled her down and interrupted her with a kiss. A slow, hungry kiss that tried to show her how much she meant to him. Kids. Now that she'd said it he wanted to start right away. A family. The Dunham-Kelleys.

He felt Declan's hand on his head, gentling him. He understood what Trick was going through. The idea of a redheaded girl with gray eyes on his shoulders, carrying both their names...

"Thank you," he murmured, reaching up to tangle his fingers with Declan's without lifting his mouth away from Jen's. "My loves."

***

"Team Jeremy, here we come." Trick grabbed her small overnight bag and loaded it into the car with his. He looked up and saw Jen in the doorway, locked in yet another Declan power kiss. He'd been on the receiving end of a few of those himself in the last hour. Professor Hot Lips really needed to give it a rest. "Damn it, Declan, I promise I'll bring her back in one piece in the morning. Just don't get so sad without us that you're tempted to take a bite of that chocolate statue. You don't want to lose all your Finn points overnight."

Jen's laughter made Declan lift his head to glare at Trick in the waning light. "I won't have time to be tempted. I called Noah while you were in the shower and he, Owen, Rory, Wyatt and Brady are all on their way over now. I thought my "TV wall" might help distract the groom. Go Team Owen."

Trick grinned. *That's my man.* "Now I'm worried. Guard the liquor with your life."

They said goodbye and Trick drove them to Stephen's house, unable to let go of Jen's hand. He couldn't stop thinking about what she'd said, letting Declan know it was all of them or none of them. It was, he realized, exactly what he'd most needed to hear.

And she wanted to have children. Even now, when she'd spent the last few months worried for her pregnant friend. Now, when she'd been dealing with reconnecting with her mother and her internship and two attention-hungry, sexually demanding men.

"I think it's going to snow again," she said, breaking the silence with a smile. "It smells like snow."

Trick inhaled and shook his head. "People say that all the time. What exactly does snow smell like?"

She opened her mouth then closed it again, thinking.

"I don't know. It smells clean, I guess. Like all the noise and smoke and grime is suddenly gone and the world is brand new again." She chuckled. "Too much cheese?"

His hand tightened on hers. "Acceptable levels for a Christmas wedding. Jen?"

"Yeah?"

He forced the words out as gently as he could. "When you're ready? We'll be good fathers."

She gasped, turning toward him in her seat. "I know that, Trick."

"We didn't have the best examples," he continued as if he hadn't heard her. "And I know your dad is a tough act to follow, but—"

"I said I know." She sounded choked up, and he didn't dare look away from the road. "There is no doubt in my mind that—when we're ready—our babies will never want for anything, and never doubt how much they're loved."

"Good." He was such a fraud. Cocky Trick. Laid back Trick. He was a big, fat phony. Tristan Dunham wanted to hold a baby in his arms. Wanted to grow old beside the only two people in the world who mattered. "I wasn't expecting that conversation. I didn't know you thought about babies." *With me.*

"Oh, Trick," she said, patting his hand playfully. "I'm a woman. I was born into this world, I cried when they spanked my ass, and then I started thinking about it."

He laughed then. He almost had to pull over because he couldn't stop and his eyes were watering. She'd used his words against him. His response to her question, "What started you thinking about ménage?"

They turned onto Stephen and Tasha's street and Trick pulled over, putting the car in park to tug her into his arms. "I love you, Jennifer Finn." He buried his face in her neck and breathed deep. "You smell like snow."

CHAPTER FIVE

Christmas Eve...

He wasn't going to make it to the wedding.

Jeremy paced the guest room Declan had put him in when he'd arrived. They'd made a big deal out of locking Owen in the library as he'd come in, reminding him every chance they got that this had been his bright idea. Tradition. No seeing the groom before the wedding. Bad luck bullshit that he'd thought sounded romantic a few days ago.

It was *not* romantic.

He'd helped Stephen get Tasha settled into their room. She wanted to argue, but it was clear she was tired from all the activity. He was so worried about her, if she argued about the wheelchair now he'd make her watch the wedding via Skype.

Jen and the others had all scattered under Ellen Finn and the wedding planner's commands, making sure they hadn't missed anything. From what little he'd seen before he was herded up the stairs to take a shower, the living room was a softly-lit winter wonderland. A damn movie set. There was even a cello.

And right now he didn't care about any of it. He needed Owen. Wanted to touch him and kiss him and make sure this was what he wanted, to let him know either way Jeremy wasn't backing out. Wedding or no wedding.

But he really wanted this wedding.

A short rap on the door had him clinging to his towel and whirling around. It was Ken. "Some bossy woman with a clipboard wants to know if you're hungry. This show doesn't start for another two hours, so you should probably have a—"

Jeremy stalked closer and lowered his voice. "I need your help."

Ken's eyebrows lifted to his hairline. "Is this bowtie help or bury a body help?" he asked cautiously.

"Because I get a little carried away with bowties and we don't have that kind of relationship."

Jeremy couldn't decide whether to glare or laugh. "This is the kind of help where you get Owen in here now and don't let anyone follow."

Ken Tanaka looked down at his shoes, his braid slipping over his shoulder as it shook with repressed laughter. "Oh," he finally responded. "*That* kind of help. I have to say I wasn't expecting this from you. Owen? Yes. Him I've been tempted to tie down since we got here. It's like mating season all the time with him isn't it? But I thought this was your idea."

Jeremy wanted to tug his hair in frustration but he couldn't drop his towel. "Please, Tanaka. It's important."

Ken nodded sharply. "Say no more, Porter. I'll be right back."

The door closed and he sat down on the bed staring at the closet where his tuxedo was hanging. It didn't feel real. The last few days with Tasha had been fun and exciting...but it hadn't really sunk in until he'd arrived.

He was marrying Owen Finn today.

Jeremy had been overwhelmed when Owen had proposed to him in front of a packed pub and his whole family. In that moment he believed he'd never be happier. He'd already been proven wrong at least a dozen times, but today might top them all. As long as Owen got his ass in this room in the next sixty seconds.

The doorknob turned and he stood, clutching his towel and trying to slow his racing heart.

"I have to get dressed, damn it, why does she wa—" Owen stopped talking to whoever was behind him when he caught sight of Jeremy. "Never mind," he spat at the looming shadow that must be Brady. "I'm good."

He slammed the door behind him, locked it and stared in silence until Jeremy dropped his towel. "Jesus," Owen groaned, swiftly untying the robe that had *Groom* stenciled on the lapel and letting it fall to the floor, revealing a body just as naked as Jeremy's. "Thank God."

Jeremy let Owen tug him close and kiss him hungrily. *Yes.* This was what he needed. Solid and real. To hell with tradition. Owen pulled back to look at him. "What do you need, babe? Having trouble getting ready without me?"

"You," Jeremy whispered, taking control and pushing Owen against the nearest wall. "I need you." He dropped to his knees and took Owen's erection deep in his mouth. Just like that first time.

"Christ, you don't know." Owen slid his fingers into Jeremy's hair, his hips already bucking forward. "I've been thinking about your mouth for days, babe. Oh fuck, like *that*. Just like that. Did you miss me that much?"

Jeremy nodded, eyes closed as lust and bliss battled for domination inside him.

"Then it's a good thing we're not doing this again. One wedding is enough for both of us." Owen's grip tightened. "God, I want to keep you on your knees all damn day for making me sleep alone, but we only have a few hours." He tugged on Jeremy's hair and hissed as he pulled out. "Where the hell is my robe?"

Don't leave, Jeremy wanted to shout, but he was too turned on. Too dazed. Why was Owen leaving?

"I believe it's my turn," Owen said, turning with the robe's tie in his hands. "Bend over the bed and put your hands behind your back, Jeremy. Now."

He didn't hesitate. This is what he needed. Owen taking control. Taking the lead. Letting him know everything was going to be fine. *Yes*—Owen tied his wrists together—better than fine.

"I have big plans for our honeymoon," Owen said conversationally. "It involves a lot of begging on your part and it's going to take days. As many hours as you thought you needed to stay away from me before the wedding."

Jesus. Longer than their session at the cabin. "Anything you want, Owen."

He felt a stinging smack on his ass cheek, and then heard a groan. "The honeymoon," Owen repeated roughly. "Not now."

Jeremy moaned low and long at the feel of the tongue between his cheeks. When it pushed inside with a growl Jeremy almost floated off the bed. "Yes," he gasped. "Owen, God that's…"

He couldn't speak anymore. His cock was digging a hole in the bed and he couldn't move with his hands tied. All he could do was take what Owen gave him. *Deeper. Fuck me, baby. I need more.* "Please."

Owen lifted his head. "Where's the—"

"Under the bed."

He bit his lip when Owen's mouth left him and then he heard rustling and wrapping paper tearing. "Who the hell gave you this?"

Jeremy pressed his forehead into the mattress. "Tasha. It was for us. For tonight."

"Fuck," Owen swore softly. "She does know her toys

and lube. I'm going to use every one of these on you after the reception. It looks like she bought out the whole store. I hope to hell you caught up on your sleep."

"I couldn't sleep without you." The honest reply was met with silence, then Owen was on the bed and cupping his face, kissing him like a man possessed.

"I need you," he gasped, pulling back and shuddering. "I need to…" He untied Jeremy's wrists and rolled him onto his back, reaching behind him for a small red bottle of lube. "I'll take my turn later. I want to see your face."

Jeremy arched his neck, writhing on the bed as Owen prepared him in silence. Then he was there, between Jeremy's spread thighs as he stretched him with a slow, delicious pressure. "Finn."

Owen gripped his wrists and held them over his head. "You'll be a Finn soon." His lips parted as he sunk further inside. "Mine."

"I'm already yours." *I've always been yours.* "Oh God…" Jeremy bent his knees and flexed his hips, needing all of him. Everything. Why was he holding back?

"Slow, Jeremy." Something in his tone made Jeremy open his eyes. "Let me love you."

And he did. Jeremy's head was spinning as Owen kissed his neck, his chest, everywhere he could reach while keeping his strokes long and deep and achingly slow.

Jeremy trembled beneath him, sounds like whimpers and pleas escaping his tight throat as the man he loved worshipped his body with a tenderness he'd rarely shown in the bedroom.

"My Jeremy," Owen whispered, pressing their foreheads together. "Always mine."

He was killing him. "I love you so damn much. Please, Owen."

Jeremy kissed him as if he were starving. It felt like he was. He was more on edge than any bondage or paddling session had ever made him. Strung out from desire with pre-cum coating the head of his cock, all he could do was wrap his legs around Owen's waist and rock himself against his tight abs. "*Owen.*"

Owen groaned against his lips, his hand slipping between them to grip as much of Jeremy's erection as he could. He changed position and slung his hips with more force—*Fuck, yes*—faster than he had before. He was close. So fucking close.

Love you, Owen. Love you, baby. Love…

"God, Jeremy." Owen was groaning loudly now. "Come for me, babe."

"*Harder*," Jeremy cried. "Please, God, don't stop. I'm going to—*Owen*."

"*Yes*." Owen's lean, beautiful body quaked against him as they came together. Jeremy wasn't sure where his orgasm ended and Owen's began. They kissed and caressed each other, shivering with each pulse of release, whispering words of praise and love.

When he came back to himself, Owen was guiding him back into the shower, gliding soapy hands lovingly over his body. He touched him with a reverence that made something tighten in Jeremy's chest. Owen rinsed him and dried him off with a towel, kissing him softly once more before stepping away to reach for his robe.

"I should go back to my room now."

Jeremy frowned. "No you shouldn't. I was wrong. This was a stupid idea."

"Yes it was." Owen laughed. "And I'm going to remind you how wrong you were until we celebrate our first anniversary. Maybe longer. But we don't want to spoil your reputation as the responsible one in this relationship, do we? Besides, my tuxedo is in the other bedroom and we both need to get dressed." He reached for the doorknob, pinning Jeremy to the spot with something painfully beautiful blazing in his Finn blue eyes. "I have a wedding to get to."

He opened the door and Jeremy saw Ken and Brady break their embrace and look guiltily in his direction. "Sorry," Brady mumbled. "You two done in there already?"

Owen snorted and walked past him without looking back. "The wedding is in an hour," he called over his shoulder. "Don't take too long with my best man."

A flushed Ken caught Jeremy's eye and sent him a stunning smile before dragging Brady away. "An hour? I can handle that."

***

"Are you ready?" Jen was holding his hand as they stood at the top of the stairs, just out of sight, listening to old Irish melodies drifting up from the cellist Declan Kelley's wedding planner had hired for the occasion.

Jeremy took a breath and squeezed her fingers gently. "I'm ready. That doesn't mean I'm not nervous."

Jen started sniffing and Jeremy shook his head. "If you start crying now, Little Finn, we're not going to make it down the stairs."

"Can't have that," Jen said with a watery laugh. "Owen would never forgive me."

"And Trick and Declan would never forgive *me* for making you cry. You look great, by the way."

Jen was wearing a gray silk dress layered with sheer silver. Her strawberry-colored hair was pulled back and tumbling in large curls down her back. She looked like an angel to Jeremy, and as she walked beside him and guests started turning in their seats to stare, she felt like one too. An angel saving him from facing this alone. He would always be a member of the Little Finn Fan Club.

From the base of the stairs, Shawn and Ellen were looking up at them, all smiles. When Ellen saw her daughter her eyes filled and she held her hand over her heart, mouthing the words, "So beautiful." Then she turned to Jeremy and that hand reached out for his. Jeremy took it and squeezed it gently.

Jen lagged behind them as Shawn gripped his shoulder in a silent statement of affection and pride. Jeremy nodded and started to move toward the dais where Owen was waiting, pausing when he realized the three of them were still walking with him. Ellen hadn't let go of his hand.

A few more steps and Stephen and Seamus were

suddenly in front of him. Their identical smiles were supportive and encouraging. They didn't say a word, just stepped aside, joining the small army of Finns gathering behind him.

Jeremy almost stumbled when he realized what was happening. The other guests—graphic artists, construction workers, pub regulars and longtime family friends—seemed to figure it out at the same time. They were all walking him down the wide aisle. Supporting him. It was the same thing they'd done after they'd found out about his relationship with Owen, only this time they were showing everyone there what they'd shown him that day. Finns stood by the people they loved. Always. No one who left here today would have any doubt that Jeremy was a welcome addition to the family. That all the Finns approved of the marriage.

Solomon and Rory showed up in front of him, patted his arm and nodded as they fell in line. Then came Noah and Wyatt. Jeremy's vision was blurring by the time he saw James stand up beside his chair. He made no move to join them, gesturing to Sol sitting beside him, staring resolutely at his shoes. Jeremy felt Shawn's hand—still on his shoulder—flex, but he didn't pause beside his brother or stop the procession. In that moment he felt sorry for Sol. He'd forgotten what it felt like to be surrounded by this much love. Shielded from harm. Jeremy covered Shawn's hand with his own, hoping he could share that feeling with Owen's father.

He got the impression of a beautiful room filled with people sitting on pristinely white chairs. The runner was cranberry red and the garland lining the aisle was a lush green. There was a giant Christmas tree in the corner of the room glowing with warm fairy lights and overflowing with small white RSVP cards signed by all the people who'd come to the wedding. It was simple, but breathtaking. He hadn't expecting anything like this.

He'd say he felt like a damn Disney princess, but Owen would never let him hear the end of it.

Owen. Jeremy looked up, but Tasha caught his eye first. She was sitting in a wheelchair wrapped with sparkling garlands, in a silver sheath dress similar to Jen's. She was radiant and smiling through her tears as he got closer to his destination.

Jeremy blinked swiftly and sought out Owen. Standing beneath an elevated bower draped in holly, mistletoe and more small sparkling lights, he stood proud and tall and so handsome Jeremy caught his breath. Brady stood beside him, his head even with the arch and his hand clutching a leash attached to the dog at his side.

He let out a short, soft laugh. Badass was wearing a Santa hat and sitting obediently beside Brady. His tail wagged furiously the instant he spotted Jeremy and Brady muttered something to the excited dog, pulling a treat from his pocket for good measure. Leave it to Owen to make Badass a groomsman.

Somewhere through the fog in his brain he heard the music change and his heart started pounding in his ears, nearly drowning it out. Almost there. Almost where I belong.

He stepped up onto the dais, Tasha momentarily squeezing his hand affectionately, and then Owen was facing him. They twined their fingers together and Jeremy tried to remember to breathe. He glanced down and chuckled again, loving the man beside him as he saw the shamrock cufflinks glittering green at his wrists.

"You like?"

He loved.

The justice of the peace they'd chosen stepped forward and the music stopped. The room was momentarily silent as they waited for her cue. "Who gives this man in marriage?"

For less than a second he thought about the parents that had kicked him out for being different. The aunt who'd hardly noticed his existence when she'd agreed to let him sleep under her roof. The loneliness.

"I do."

"I do."

"We do."

"I do."

Shawn chuckled. "I think we all do. We're his family."

Jeremy heard several soft sobs at that, unsure of where they were coming from but agreeing with the sentiment. He couldn't have imagined... But he shouldn't be surprised. Nothing this wonderful family did could surprise him ever again.

"You may be seated," the justice said, beaming at Owen and Jeremy as the family found their seats.

She set down the book she'd been holding and clasped her hands in front of her while Jeremy's gaze clung to Owen's. "We've come together today to join two souls together in marriage. But I think we've all just seen that this union is particularly blessed, and that there are more souls involved than we can count. The couple's family and friends have shown their unconditional love and support with their actions and their words, and I know we all join them in their joy for this occasion. It's hard not to root for Owen Finn and Jeremy Porter when you get to know them. The city has been captivated for weeks. Personally, I don't think it has to do with Owen's brother or the gender of his fiancé as much as it has to do with their story. A simple, but powerful story about two good men and the close, unflinching friendship they've shared for more than half of their lives. Without planning or expectation, that friendship blossomed with the fullness of time into so much more than either of them ever dreamed. And it brought them here before us today."

Jeremy had dreamed. He'd just never imagined his dream had a chance in hell of coming true. Owen's crystal blue eyes were dark with emotion that matched his own as she continued. "There are many kinds of love—each one a gift that makes life worthwhile. The love of a parent for their child. The love of siblings and friends. And a love like the one Owen and Jeremy share. A love that demands to be acknowledged and celebrated, because it cannot be denied when witnessed." She smiled and turned in his direction. "I believe Jeremy has something he wants to say."

Jeremy's throat went instantly dry. He licked his lips, feeling a flutter of panic. He'd written something he'd thought was good and memorized it, but everything had flown out of his head the second he'd gotten to the stairs. After his proposal, Jeremy knew Owen deserved a public declaration of his own. Now he only hoped he hadn't lost the ability to speak. And that his heart knew what to say.

"Owen—" He swallowed past the frog in his throat and started again. "Owen, I've loved you for as long as I can remember. And I remember everything. That first day you invited me over to your house after school, when your mother insisted on feeding me and got out her sewing kit without saying a word after she saw a hole in my shirt. I remember when you showed your dad my sketchbook at the dinner table and he told me I had real talent. That we were having so much fun you asked if I could stay the night, and when she realized there was no one I needed to call to ask permission, your mother said I was welcome anytime, whether you were home or not." He saw Owen's lips subtly wobble as he glanced down at his family and he knew Ellen was crying. "I remember that you gave me the world and you didn't even know it. Proud parents who worried about me, a little sister who was more than happy to let me spoil her rotten, and two older brothers I couldn't help but admire. And you, a best friend who is the star of every good memory I have. You taught me how to laugh at myself, never once judged me for my life choices and always had my back, right or wrong. How could I not have loved you?"

Jeremy took a breath, feeling Owen's fingers clutching his. "But what I thought was love back then is nothing compared to what I feel for you now. After all those years of you being my constant, you suddenly turned everything upside down without warning and made me happier than I knew it was possible to be. You are the love of my life and you never have to imagine walking through this world without me. I'll always be at your side and on your side."

He heard Brady's muttered, "*Damn*" a second before Owen yanked him into his arms and kissed him, right there in front of everyone.

"Son, she didn't tell you to kiss him yet," Shawn called from the front row, causing a ripple of warm laughter to flow over the room.

"No one has to tell me when to kiss him," Owen responded gruffly, but he took a step back, still holding Jeremy's hands. "Is it my turn to talk?"

Jeremy knew Owen hated giving speeches. He hadn't wanted to write any vows or speak at the wedding, insisting he'd already said everything during his proposal. Apparently he'd changed his mind. There was a moment's fear that blowjobs would be mentioned, but it disappeared as soon as he opened his mouth. "I won't try to top that. I will never be as good with words as you are. But with you I don't have to be. You already know me. You always have. I'm not sure I deserve that heart you've given to me, but I'm not giving it back. And knowing me the way you do, you know that I'll spend the rest of our lives together trying to earn it." He tilted his head toward the justice. "Let's say these vows so I can kiss my husband again."

Jeremy vaguely heard himself repeating the words. Love, honor and cherish. Sickness and health and forsaking all others. He heard Owen promise the same in a low, reverent tone. The rings he'd picked out went on and then there was cheering as Owen kissed him again, pulling his head down and making him forget his own name.

Hands clapped his back and arms engulfed him as they pulled him away from Owen's side. Jeremy turned from Noah to see Stephen on his knees beside Tasha's wheelchair, his arm around her as she sobbed. He knelt down and kissed her hand. "You hanging in there, best woman?"

"Barely," she choked out. "My baby is *married*. It was so beautiful."

Stephen shrugged as if to blame her emotion on the pregnancy, but his eyes were suspiciously bright when he gripped Jeremy's arm. "Proud of you both."

Jeremy rubbed something out of his eye that was *not* a tear and kissed Tasha on the forehead. "No dancing now. Those little ones need their rest."

"If Rory had gotten me a motorized wheelchair the way I asked him to, I wouldn't promise anything." She smiled up at him weakly and then started crying again. "I hate hormones. And I think the babies need cake."

"Not until we have pictures." Jen appeared beside them, her face glowing and a compact in her hand. "Back up brothers, I'm the best woman's official touch up girl."

"Yes." Tasha pushed Jeremy and Stephen away. "And I'm standing for some of the pictures so deal with it and don't try and stop me."

Jeremy felt Owen's hand slide back into his and he smiled in relief, allowing himself to be led away. He wasn't sure how many pictures were taken or who they took them with, though he did remember that Trick had to snag the leash from Brady and run when Badass started to whine.

"Don't forget to put on his booties," Owen called, and the Finn men teased him mercilessly until the photographer said it was time to cut the cake.

Owen kissed his cheek. "Declan didn't get cake," he murmured. "Apparently really, disgustingly rich people like to get creative with their chocolate."

"Holy shit," Jeremy said, stunned as a life-size replica of the vigilante demon from his bestselling comic book series was wheeled out in front of him. It was made entirely of chocolate. White, dark and milk. He glanced at Jen's boyfriend for a second before his gaze returned to the piece of art. "Holy shit, Declan."

Owen slid an arm around his waist. "He had them make tiny pizzas for me, too. Very upscale, but I'll need at least twenty to tide me over. The professor is good at sucking up."

Declan snorted. "I'm standing right here."

"You're standing on the top ten list of my favorite people at the moment." Owen's voice was charm itself. "So don't go changing."

He saw Seamus grab his twins, Penny and Wes, as they ran full tilt for the statue, their legs bicycling wildly in the air. "You need to wait, guys," he said with a patient smile. "This isn't Willy Wonka's, it's your uncle's wedding."

"It's Vini, Dad!" Wes cried. "Uncle Jer, look, it's Vini!"

Jeremy beamed. Five-year-old Wes wasn't old enough to be into comics, but he'd seen some framed art when they'd come to visit and demanded to know everything about the strange little character that lived in Jeremy's head. He wouldn't stop talking about it. The adorable towhead would be pleased to know he was getting his own framed drawing of the demon on an adventure with Wes and his twin sister for Christmas.

Right now, however, chocolate was all Wes wanted. "Jake," Seamus called. "Can you grab one of these sugar addicts?"

"When can we ditch this party?" Owen asked after distracting him by nuzzling his neck while the photographer circled them, snapping one shot after the other. "After we cannibalize that statue?"

"This is our party, Owen." Jeremy laughed quietly, still watching Seamus trying to wrangle his children. His older son, Jake, had stepped in to help at his father's request. "We can't ditch our own wedding reception."

"You shouldn't tell him he can't do things." Jeremy turned to see Rory grinning at them with two strange men beside him. "You know he thinks the word is a dare."

Owen stood behind Jeremy, wrapping his arms around his waist and resting his chin on his shoulder. "Pot meet Kettle," he said lazily, practically purring against Jeremy like a contented lion. "Introduce us to your friends."

Jeremy saw a warning in Rory's eyes before his smile widened and he slid his arms through both of theirs. "Rig and David? This is my cousin Owen and his new husband Jeremy."

Rig was not as tall as he was bulked up with muscle. With his Roman nose and dark hair he was definitely attractive, but he was eyeing them as if they were on the auction block at Owen's favorite BDSM club. "Pleasure to meet you. And congratulations." His words were polite, but his eyes were anything but. He was as sexual as Rory. No wonder they were friends.

The other man was different. Gorgeous, his tall, muscular frame had a more "naturally gifted" feeling.

Very hot boy next door. Jeremy saw Rory steal a glance at his friend as though waiting for his reaction. "Nice to meet you both," he said politely. "I'm David Mills. Sorry we horned in on your special day, but we've been hearing about this wedding for months and couldn't resist when Rory called to invite us."

"He talks about us," Owen faux-whispered to Jeremy. "And you thought he didn't like us."

"You're a conversation starter, that's all," Rory said with a smirk. "My proof that no man is a straight line." His gaze flickered to David's again.

What was *that* about?

"So true," Owen agreed easily. "We *are* fascinating. Tell us how you know Rory, David."

Brown eyes looked momentarily startled. "Oh. Well, we met in our senior year of high school. I was a transfer student and Rory took pity on the new kid." He smiled at his friend. "He was all about school spirit back then. Everyone loved their mascot, so I had an easier time adjusting."

But Jeremy frowned, suddenly realizing how little he knew about Brady's brothers. At least, the lives they led between Finn Agains. They needed to fix that. He needed to fix that. "Mascot?"

Rory dug his elbow into David's side. "Thanks for that."

"College," Rig joined the conversation, pointing to himself. "Back when Rory stopped being a mascot and became the campus wild child."

"Then you're practically family." Jeremy was having a hard time forming sentences since Owen's hand had drifted down to cup his behind. "You probably know half the people here."

Rory looked uncomfortable, pulling at the collar of his dress shirt. "Noah and Wyatt. But they won't be staying long enough to meet everyone else."

David sent him a strange look Jeremy couldn't decipher. "We're not in that much of a hurry. I don't have to be anywhere until brunch with my parents tomorrow."

"That's good," Owen said, the smirk in his voice clear. "Flexibility is important in a friendship. If you can't *bend*, you can't friend. Right Rory?"

Rory seemed to know what he was talking about. He flinched and sent his cousin a withering glare. "You would know, Owen. Come on, guys. Let's leave the newlyweds alone. I'm thirsty." He tugged his friends away a little too forcefully.

"Have fun," Owen called after them sweetly as they disappeared toward the champagne fountain. Jeremy sighed. They had a champagne fountain. Tequila would have been more appropriate.

"Are you going to tell me what I missed there?" Jeremy asked suspiciously. "I only left you alone for two days."

Owen turned him around and sent him a sensual smile. "I'll tell you if you come upstairs with me."

He made a face. "Owen, we can't—"

"Rory's right, can't is a dare,'" he insisted. "And we'll be back before anyone knows we're gone. I love you and I believe I promised to consummate the hell out of that ass." He saw Jeremy's lips twitch and pressed. "It *is* traditional, husband."

He wasn't wrong.

CHAPTER SIX

Seamus Finn

Christmas Day...

"But *why*?"

Seamus tweaked his daughter's bright red nose. "Because people don't marry blood relations."

Penny put her hands on her hips. "Why?"

"Because then you can't have babies." The lie slipped from his lips out of self-preservation. This conversation was way too complicated for a five-year-old. Or the father of a five-year-old.

She scrunched up her face thoughtfully, looking adorably annoyed. "Jake and I have different blood, right? He had a different dad before you. So we *could* have babies if we wanted to." She looked so relieved he wanted to laugh.

Seamus sighed and whistled for his brother's dog again. "Come on, Lucky Penny. We need to grab Bad and get inside."

She placed her gloved hand in his obediently. "That's not his name, Daddy. And good. I'm cold and stockings were *hours* ago, but Gram said we had to wait."

"Gram is right." Not always, he silently amended, but often enough. They'd all stayed overnight at Declan Kelley's hotel-sized house so they could spend Christmas together. Since it was the season of peace and love, when his mother sat him down this morning and asked him to forgive her for not practicing what she preached, he capitulated easily. After the outpouring of love at the wedding, it was hard not to. And he'd noticed Jen and his mother holding each other as Owen and Jeremy exchanged their vows. If his baby sister could start fresh after what happened, so could Seamus.

It bothered him more than he'd thought it would, her treatment of Jennifer. He was as shocked as anyone when Solomon told him the family secret. Stunned because he'd never had a clue. But that wasn't what truly upset him. After the blind acceptance she gave to Owen and Stephen—hell, to him the first time he came home with a son that wasn't his—he couldn't wrap his head around the guilt she'd nearly buried her only girl under. When he realized how complicit he and the others had been by not seeing Jen as a grown woman—not noticing how unhappy she'd been before—he felt pretty damn bad about himself as a brother. And disappointed in his mother for the first time in his life.

He looked down at Penny. He was a protective father too, and there was nothing he wouldn't do to keep her from harm and heartbreak. But he hoped he'd never load her down with his personal baggage. The last thing he wanted was for her to be afraid to take a chance on love because she'd learned the wrong lessons from him.

"I think I'll ask Gram."

"Ask her what, angel?" Seamus finally saw the dog and whistled one more time. Hopefully he'd listen. Penny had been holding the leash when Badass bolted away in the snow, booties and all.

"I bet she thinks it'd be okay if I wedded Jake."

"Married Jake. And I bet you're wrong. Don't bother Gram with that right now. It's Christmas." He'd become more open-minded about a lot of things this year, but he drew the line at letting her marry her brother.

Penny muttered under her breath, her little legs stomping beside his.

"What?"

"I want a chocolate state."

Seamus snorted. "Statue."

"That's what I said. And a Jell-O."

That one took him a minute. "Do you mean a cello? As in the instrument?"

"I said that, Daddy."

Badass stopped beside them, panting happily with his leash dragging behind him. He grabbed it then picked Penny up in his arms. "We can get you a chocolate statue and cello lessons, I promise. But let's save the wedding talk for a while. Until you're twenty-five."

"But I love him. And everyone says when you love someone you're supposed to get wedded." Her breath made clouds in the air and her big blue eyes made her look like a doll. She was so precious.

"Married. And of course you love him, Penny. He's your family. Remember what the justice of the peace said? There are different kinds of love."

"Was your married that nice?"

"Wedding?" He kept his tone casual. "Penny you know I never had a wedding. I told you that last night."

And last week. And the week before that. She'd gone just as crazy over the wedding plans as her grandmother. It brought up a lot of hard questions.

Penny nodded, sucking in her lower lip. "She had to move far away and take care of herself."

She was talking about her mother. "That's right. But you have Gram and Aunt Jen and Aunt Tasha. And they're not moving anywhere, I promise. Now are you ready to open some presents?"

Like a flipped switch her mood changed and she wriggled wildly in his arms until he set her down. Her snow boots were a little too big and she waddled precariously as she ran toward the door. "Hurry! Wes will open everything without us."

Jake wouldn't let him, Seamus knew. Not until she got there. He was a good big brother. Always the one she turned to if she was hurt or had a question she didn't want to ask her father. Jake never complained. Sometimes Seamus worried he'd put too much pressure on him, relied on him too much. But he'd always been so damn thoughtful. A wise old man trapped in a child's body. He hoped that wasn't what he wanted to see. He prayed Jake wasn't hiding unhappiness beneath that shy, serious demeanor.

Stop worrying about the kids for a minute and enjoy the day.

How many times had his mother said that to him? Before Tasha's pregnancy took a turn, Stephen often said the same thing. That he needed to spend time with people outside the pub and his own four walls. Adult people. That he needed to talk about something besides beer and finger painting.

But he couldn't complain. His life was a good one. He owned his own business and was raising four interesting, creative and compassionate kids. They kept him hopping and didn't leave much time for anything else.

It was perfectly normal for him to feel a little lonely now and then. Especially after *that* wedding. He wasn't made of stone and his siblings had all found someone, or multiple someone's—he corrected with a small, reflexive wince—to share their lives with. It was natural to quietly wonder what it felt like to have a partner you could depend on that much. Someone you were that passionate about.

Normal. Natural. Now shake it the hell off.

He looked down at the booted dog. "Do you know that song, Badass? Jake loves it. Shake it off," he crooned, shouting in surprise when the snow beast shook his coat and ice hit him square in the face. Apparently Owen knew that song too.

The door slammed open and Penny leaned outside. "Daddy! Presents!"

"Coming." *I was just singing to a dog about my problems.* "Close the door now, I don't want to pay Aunt Jen's electric bill."

He hung his coat up and took off the dog's insulated waterproof slippers before he let him join the crowd in the warm living room. When Seamus reached the kitchen, Owen and Jeremy were making out by the coffee machine. "Stop already. The wedding's over. You're old news."

Owen turned toward him, his cheeks flushed. "Exactly. We're married now. We don't have to restrain ourselves."

Seamus grabbed his chest dramatically. "You were restraining yourselves *before*?"

Brady stalked into the room with a scowl, sliding his phone into his pocket. Uh-oh. "Trouble?" He hoped not. Between Burke and that slave club or whatever Brady had been working on, there'd been too much trouble this year. He had kids to worry about.

Brady looked down and nodded. "Damn right there's trouble. That morning show girl Owen and Jeremy invited to the wedding? What was her name?"

"Casey? Cassidy?" Seamus couldn't remember. He didn't watch her show.

Brady shrugged, agitated. "Noah took off with her in the middle of the wedding. Her station has been calling Stephen's office because she's not answering her phone, and Noah's is still turned off."

"Shit," Owen groaned, stepping out of Jeremy's arms. "That can't be good."

Brady sighed. "It's my fault. I should have made them all promise to behave themselves at the reception. Noah is just the latest news. Last night, Wyatt got caught in the pantry with the caterer's assistant—his daughter no less. Rory apparently frenched one of his buddies in front of Elder—"

"Wait." Owen held up his hand. "Rory kissed David? In front of your father?"

"How did you know his name?" Brady ran a hand through his hair. "And yeah. I'm not sure how you missed it. Sol tried to leave without talking to anyone and had some harsh words for Rory when he tried to stop him. The mistletoe was right there so I guess he decided his cousin's wedding was a great place to prove a point. With his tongue. It went downhill from there."

"I must have missed that too." Seamus shook his head. "All I remember is following the kids around all night and falling asleep with my shoes on. Ah, to be young." He paused. "Solomon didn't do anything crazy did he?"

Brady chuckled. "I wish. He's already gone too. Merry damn Christmas."

"Well hell. Let's go before we lose anyone else," Seamus said, already moving toward the living room. "Wes and Little Sean aren't good at restraint. Let's at least watch them open their presents before we all scatter to the wind again."

They were horrible at restraint, Seamus thought as he stared at the carnage of torn wrapping paper and ravaged bows littering the floor around them. The couches were back, he thought gratefully as he sunk into one beside Brady's boyfriend Ken. "Those are their presents right?" Seamus tried to smile. "No one else is missing anything?"

Ken laughed and patted his leg. "Your mother took matters into her own hands after Solomon and James went after Noah. She was the one passing out the gifts."

He'd been planning to take pictures of the whole family together. Damn. "Good." He glanced down at little Sean and grinned despite his mood. The child's excitement was infectious. "What did Santa bring you, Sean?"

"Uncle Necky! Candy!"

Oh joy. Seamus raised his eyebrow at Ken Tanaka. "Nice. Santa doesn't care about future dental bills, I'm guessing."

"Dad?" Jake's voice sounded surprised so he looked up.

"What is it, Jake?"

"It's Santa."

Seamus tilted his head. "What about him?"

Jake walked up to him, holding a wide, rectangular box as if it contained dynamite. "It looks like he got you something."

Ken leaned forward. "Mrs. Finn? I think it's time for you and the kids to find the special present I got for them in the garage."

Seamus felt his jaw drop when his mother smiled sweetly and stood without argument, guiding his children away like the pied piper of grandmothers. Jake hesitated.

"Go on, son." Seamus smiled encouragingly. "I'll show you later."

What was going on here? He looked around the room at all the overly innocent faces. Jen was sitting on the floor with Trick and Declan, all of them spoiling Badass with attention as they gathered up the wrapping paper. Owen, Jeremy, Stephen and Tasha were on the couch opposite, watching him with undisguised interest.

Brady and Wyatt were standing behind Shawn, and Ken's foot was tapping restlessly beside him as he held the box. "Anyone want to fill me in here?"

"Open it," Owen said quickly, frowning when Jeremy tugged him back against his chest. "I didn't say anything."

Oh well. Seamus supposed he couldn't hope for a carboy with the shape of this box, but then, none of them knew anything about making beer so he shouldn't be surprised.

He unwrapped it slowly, wondering what they thought warranted this kind of attention. And who exactly was his mystery Santa? He lifted the box's lid and looked inside cautiously, sifting through the contents.

Brochures for tourist attractions and breweries. A bright green travel guide. A credit card and a round-trip airline ticket in his name. "Ireland? Who the hell got me a ticket to *Ireland*?"

"We got tickets too," Owen said, obviously unable to resist sharing the news. "I love our broken down cabin and I had big plans for it, but a honeymoon in Ireland sounds too good to pass up."

Seamus felt a headache coming on. "Let's see if I've got this straight. For Christmas, *Santa* is sending me to Ireland as the third wheel on my brother's honeymoon? Does Santa expect me to keep them in line? Is this a gift or payback for something they think I've done?"

Brady scowled. "It's an all-expenses paid vacation to another country, Seamus. Not a travel mug. Don't be a dick."

"You're right," he agreed readily, still floored. "But I obviously can't use it. This is nearly three weeks of being away from home and," He squinted at the dates. "Almost three months in the future?"

"That's when your friend in Galway has a clear enough schedule to show you the sights and take you through the brewing process."

Seamus stilled, turning his head to study Ken

suspiciously. "My friend in Galway?" Was the infamous hacker monitoring his emails?

"You mentioned it to me," Jen intervened swiftly, sensing his suspicions. "That you've been swapping emails with a brewer in Ireland? It was easy to get the email, Seamus. It's right on their website."

His interest in travel had suddenly increased over the last sixty seconds. God, it would be amazing to go. How better to learn the best way to incorporate brewing into the pub than learning from the masters? He shook his head. Impossible. There was no way it was going to happen. "Three months from now the kids are in school and I'm swamped at the pub or in parent-teacher meetings. Three months from now the weather might be good enough for me to patch that leak on my porch roof. Three months from n—"

"Three months from now you're going to Ireland, Seamus Finn. That's final." His father was watching him with his arms crossed, a mulish expression on his face.

"No, Dad. I'm not." He could be stubborn too.

How dare someone try to send him on a vacation to talk about beer in Ireland? It's not like it was his dream come true or anything.

"Your mother and I will take care of the children. Jen

and the others will help out wherever they can. Brady and Ken have already agreed to look after the pub while you're away. Under my supervision, naturally."

Seamus glanced at Brady. "You're willing to put in that kind of time?"

"We're insisting," Ken corrected beside him.

He lifted his hands helplessly. "But Owen and Jeremy are—"

Shawn put his hands on his knees and leaned forward. It was his father's body language for meaning business. "They'll be touring castles and enjoying themselves. You'll be on your own for everything but the flight there and back. But while you're there…"

Here we go.

"We have a cousin or two in Galway I'd like you to look up for me. It might be nice to get to know those Finns before I die."

There it was. When Shawn Finn asked you to do something for him "before he died", there was simply no way to refuse him. He never had to scream or shout. Never had to threaten. Because he rarely asked for anything, he got whatever he wanted.

Seamus couldn't think of another argument, anyway. He'd miss the kids, sure but… He wanted to go. "It's too much." Everyone groaned and he shook his head. "I didn't say I wasn't going. I'm clearly going. But it's still too much."

"You're too much, brother." Stephen pressed his wife's shoulder to his head and caressed her temple when she closed her eyes. Seamus hoped she wasn't too worn out from the last few days. "You give the actual shirt off your back to complete strangers, rescue damsels in distress... You have enough points in your ledger to officially apply for sainthood. But you suck at accepting gifts."

"It's Christmas." Jen hopped up to sit on his lap, crushing the box while she kissed his cheek the way she used to as a child. The way Penny did now when she wanted something. "And it's your turn to have an adventure. So just say thank you and start planning your trip."

He laughed, but his throat was tight with suppressed emotion. He was a lucky man with a full life. Blessed with family. "Thank you. And Merry Christmas, Santa. I owe you one. Probably more than one. A vacation from all my cares sounds too good to be true."

No cares at all? What the hell will I do with myself?

CHAPTER SEVEN

January 15th

"I'm cold."

Stephen held her hand and blew on it. "I know baby."

"And I'm sick of ice chips. Why can I have ice chips, but not water? Is science not a prerequisite for the medical profession?"

Her husband was smiling at her as proudly as if she'd just recited the entire Bill of Rights from memory. She wanted to hit him for being this nice and looking this good right now. His hair was slightly more mussed than usual and the Finn Club t-shirt Seamus made for him was wrinkled—a far cry from all the perfectly pressed suits in their closet. Unfortunately, it only made him look sexier. As if he'd just rolled out of bed after having great sex. Tasha had gotten a glimpse of herself in a hallway mirror when they wheeled her into her private room in the maternity ward, and she'd almost screamed. Her hair had taken on a life of its own, shaping itself to the cap she'd worn for the procedure. Birds could nest and she would never know.

"Is she up for company?" Jeremy's voice came from behind the door where she could see a stuffed bear waving a white flag of surrender.

"No," she snapped grumpily. "Not unless you're my hairdresser or lasagna." She took another look at the bear and gave in. "Or my Jeremy."

Stephen nodded his greeting as Jeremy clapped him on the back. "The anesthesia's worn off but they just put in a morphine drip. She'll feel better soon."

Tasha glared at her husband, but didn't pull away. She liked what he was doing too much. "Will I? How do you know, Senator? Did you have your stomach split open and nearly twelve pounds of Finn scooped out today?"

Jeremy winced, but moved closer and took her other hand gently in his, carefully avoiding the tape and needles. "Stephen texted us right away but we couldn't see you until you got into this private suite. Everyone's in the waiting room."

Dear Lord. "Everyone?"

"No reporters and the Baby Bump Brigade has that restraining order, so not everyone," Jeremy teased. "But the family is here. We were too excited to wait for the news at home."

Too worried. He didn't say it but she knew it was true. She never wanted to put anyone through that again. It was a nightmare, having so little control of her life. Being helpless. Driving her new husband nuts with all her temper tantrums and not being able to help with most of her best friend's wedding. "You're still on your honeymoon."

"Pre-honeymoon," Jeremy corrected, a bemused smile curving his lips. "The real thing isn't for another month and a half. Owen still has to get his passport." He paused and bit his lip. "How are you feeling?"

Shit. She knew that look. She really did look bad. She forced herself to smile at Jeremy. "Sweetheart, I love you, you know that. But I need you to leave and get Little Finn. I think my overnight bag is still in the car. Give it to her and send her in. Stephen can you give him the keys?"

Her husband obeyed instantly, still not moving from his spot beside her as he reached for his jacket. But Jeremy hesitated. "No one cares how you look, Tasha. You just gave birth to two—"

"LF AT FOUR!" Tasha said, louder than she'd intended to. "Sorry, we don't have a code for needing a touch up and I'm desperate. Go, Jeremy. If you love me, then make it fast."

Call her vain, but there was no way in hell she was letting the entire Finn clan parade into her hospital room and gawk at the wildebeest she'd become. "I'm sorry, Stephen."

He frowned, mystified. "For what?"

"I'm being awful. I look like a screenshot of a horror movie and I'm not exactly a glowing beacon of maternal Zen."

He kissed her fingertips and looked into her eyes. "Natasha Finn, you just gave me the greatest gift of my life. You've made me a father of two healthy—"

"Don't tell me," she interrupted him, panicking. "I haven't seen them yet."

She'd been upset about that too. She'd heard stories about husbands holding the babies near the new mother's heads so they could bond while they were being sewn back up, but she'd been having some trouble and the babies had a few of their own. "You said healthy? They're healthy?"

"Two strong, healthy babies. They just need some extra TLC before they were ready for their debut. But the doctor says everything is fine now. They're fine. I never doubted it for a minute, because they're part of you. Part of us. And as far as I'm concerned you're a goddess and you can behave anyway you want. Have anything you want."

"Tea?"

He tried not to smile. "Ice chips."

"Lies. You're an evil, lying politician with sexy bedroom eyes and a kinky side I couldn't resist. And *now* look at me."

He didn't even flinch. "You love me."

She hated it when he was right.

Jen came rushing in with her bag in hand and Tasha nearly wept. She sent Stephen into the hallway—the first time he'd stopped being agreeable all day—and let Jen work a brush through her knotted curls and wrestle the angry hair into an acceptable bun. After that all she needed, according to Jen, was a little lip-gloss. She felt like a new woman.

Or maybe the morphine had kicked in.

When Stephen came back inside he wasn't alone. Her in-laws were right behind him. Ellen and Shawn stood at the edge of her bed, grinning at her in a way that made her cheeks heat. She couldn't begrudge them this visit. They'd been wonderful, and she already knew they were the best grandparents on the planet. Wes and Penny Finn took every opportunity to tell her so.

Stephen took her hand again. "They're bringing them in, Natasha. I'm going to put another pillow behind you."

"My babies?"

God, he was such a beautiful man when he smiled. He still made her damn knees wobble, and she wasn't even standing up. "Thank you, Senator Sexy."

Shawn's chuckle drifted up from her feet. "Medicine's working. That's good."

She laughed with him, tipsy from her sudden lack of discomfort. "It's about damn time."

Jen was still beside her and Tasha reached up and patted her arm. "Someone needs to apologize to Jeremy. My hair chased him out of the room."

"He understands." Jen looked toward the door and

smiled, her hand coming up to cover her mouth. "Oh my God, Tasha. They're here."

She watched as if outside her body. The nurse handed a blanketed bundle to Stephen, who looked up at his father with tears in his eyes, asking for help with the second.

Jen moved out of the way as her father took her place beside Tasha and Stephen joined her on the other. She saw a tiny fist escape one pile as if to check the temperature before disappearing again.

They lowered her babies carefully onto her chest. Her arms instinctively cradled them as she took in their scrunched up faces. They looked profoundly pissed off to be out of the safe warm room they'd spent the last eight months in.

They were already taking after her.

She knew she was crying. She could feel the tears on her cheeks as she blinked away the blur so she could see them more clearly. Her babies. Stephen's babies. She looked up at him, smiling. "Boys?"

He brushed his knuckle tenderly over her damp cheek. "How can you tell?"

She cuddled them closer and they seemed to like it. Maybe they were hungry. "I'm their mother. Plus, these blue blankets were a fairly big clue."

Ellen slipped into her husband's arms after a few minutes, staring raptly at her treasures and Tasha knew what she wanted. "Would you like to hold one of your grandsons?"

"Twin boys, Shawn. Honey, look how perfect they are."

"They look exactly like Stephen and Seamus," he said proudly.

Jen snorted. "They don't look like anybody yet, Dad. And I'm still hoping they take after me. We need a matching set of redheads."

Ellen carefully lifted the tiny body in her arms and asked what they'd decided to name them.

Tasha's smile was innocent. She hoped Stephen remembered the plan they'd come up with months ago. "Well for a boy, I was thinking about Huckleberry. Huck for short."

Stephen caressed the cheek of the one she was still holding with his finger, sending her a subtle wink. "And *I* was thinking about Boris. Every Natasha should have one."

Ellen Finn was silent for a minute, hugging the baby closer as if to protect him from his parents and their horrible ideas. "Huck Finn?" she asked faintly. "You want to name my grandchildren Huck and Boris Finn?"

Tasha laughed, but flinched when she felt a sharp pinch in her stomach. "We're teasing. Though I can't swear that one's nickname won't be Huckleberry, because look at him. He's so sweet."

Stephen kissed Tasha's forehead and spoke without taking his eyes from his child. "We liked the name Patrick, for Natasha's father." She felt the smallest tinge of sadness that he wasn't standing next to the Stephen's parents and studying his grandchildren. She wanted him to know about them. To know how complete her life had just become. *You will never doubt my love*, she promised her boys silently. *And whether you like it or not? I will never leave you.*

"And, if it's okay with you," Stephen looked up at his father somberly. "Edward—Ned—for your father."

Tasha worried for a moment that they'd made a mistake. Shawn's blue eyes were instantly drowning in tears he refused to shed. She knew the stories. Ned Finn was connected to the Irish mob and Sol and Shawn had both renounced their ties to him. Sol became police chief and spent his life obsessed with rebuilding the tarnished Finn name. Shawn moved forward and found happiness in his family. But for some reason Seamus believed he might like it.

"It's okay if you don't like the idea. We were also thinking of—"

"No." Shawn interrupted her by reaching down to grip her hand. "Ned is good, Natasha," he said in a gravelly voice. "Ned is exactly right."

Jen leaned over Stephen's shoulder and smiled. "Hi, Ned." She looked up at the baby her mother was holding and her smile turned mischievous. "Hey there, Huckleberry."

Her mother shook her head, but she laughed. "I think you should have your baby back while you can, Tasha." She handed Patrick over tenderly. "Shawn and I will go out and let Seamus have a turn. He's climbing the walls out there, waiting to see his brother's sons. But we won't be far."

Ellen slipped her arm through Shawn's and was speaking in a soft, soothing voice as she led him out, Jen close behind. "Should we think of another name?" Tasha asked Stephen, unsure. "The last thing I want is to have his grandfather cry every time the little guy enters the room. We liked Henry too, didn't we?"

Stephen picked Ned up and smiled at her. "I don't

think we need to change a thing. Seamus was right. Dad's missed his father, the family he grew up with, for a while now. A boy needs his father, don't you, Ned?"

"And his mother," Tasha whispered against Patrick's soft forehead. "You're my Huckleberry."

Stephen laughed "Does our son's nickname have anything to do with that old Wyatt Earp movie you've been watching on a loop?"

Tasha blushed. "I only had a few movies on my tablet and I was stuck in bed a lot. Alone, with only poor, sick-but-still-sexy Doc Holiday to keep me company."

"Sexy?"

"Don't be jealous."

"I'm not jealous," Stephen assured her cockily. "I know you're mine. You wouldn't sweep me aside for some long-dead dentist with a bad cough."

She laughed carefully as the door opened again, Seamus and his son Jake peering around the door. "Are we interrupting?"

Stephen beamed at him and Tasha hid her smile by nuzzling Ned's temple. He was so overjoyed and proud it made her giddy. It made her want ten more…but she was sure that would pass. These two were going to be a handful as it was.

She looked up to watch Seamus pulling Stephen into a tight bear hug, practically lifting his twin off the ground. "Welcome to fatherhood," he said with a slight hitch in his voice. "You'll never sleep again."

Stephen laughed as his brother set him down and patted him on the back. Tasha caught Jake's eye and rolled hers. "As if he made them all by himself."

Jake pushed his dark hair out of his eyes and smiled shyly at her. "You like them?"

Oh damn, the hormones were still raging. Tasha swallowed hard. "I love them Jake. In a few years they'll be sick of me because I don't plan to let them out of my sight." Or my arms.

Jake digested this, nodded, and moved closer. She saw Seamus turn away and wipe his hand over his eyes, composing himself. These weren't the first newborns young Jake had come to visit, Tasha thought about Penny, Wes and Little Sean. But she might be the first mother he knew who wanted to keep them.

"What do you think of your cousins, Jake?" Tasha gave him an encouraging smile. "I hope you like them, because I was hoping you'd show them the ropes. Our family can be a little confusing." *And I'd love it if they were both as sweet as you.*

"I can do that," Jake said with a quiet confidence that belied his age. Nearly thirteen, but he might as well be thirty. She hoped he found time to be a kid before he graduated high school.

"Of course he can." Seamus had himself together and was gazing at his son with pride. "Jake is a Finn, isn't he?" Not biologically, but Tasha knew firsthand that blood wasn't the only thing that mattered to this family.

Stephen's brother choked up again when he picked Ned up in his arms. "They're smaller than Penny was when she was born. So precious."

Ned's fist thrust out of his blanket again and a tiny hand curled around his uncle's finger. "Strong grip," Seamus laughed. "Ned might be a scrapper like his namesake. Or his Aunt Jen."

Tasha grinned. "As long as he doesn't pursue a life of crime I'll be happy."

Seamus met Tasha's gaze with eyes so like his brothers—so full of love and pride—that she felt her breath catch. "You'd never let that happen. Not to these two angels."

"No, I wouldn't."

He glanced over at his brother. "I forgot how good newborn babies smell. It doesn't last long, so enjoy it.

And if you ever need someone to babysit…"

Tasha held up her free hand. "We'll find someone else, because you'll be in Ireland doing boring, manly things like making beer."

Jake's laugh was quiet but infectious. "Tough luck, Dad. You'll miss out on all the fun."

She hoped not. If anyone needed fun it was Seamus. Good, X-rated, completely adult fun that babies had no business being around. Her brother-in-law needed to shake off his case of *the dads* and remember what being single felt like. Her only fear was that he would stay in that brewery all day, surrounded by old Irish men and ignoring his baser urges.

Stephen took Ned from Seamus and winked at Jake. "That's right. We'll be here, up to our elbows in diapers and feedings and your poor father will be all alone on the other side of the ocean, waiting for us to call and share every detail." He shrugged, but his eyes were sparkling. "Sometimes you just have to suffer through life's trials and tribulations. In Ireland."

Seamus sent his brother a look meant to silence him, then gestured subtly to Jake. "Let's give them some peace before the next group of visitors come knocking."

"I love you, brother," Stephen said softly, the words

thick with emotion.

"I love you too, Stephen. You did good."

Tasha bit her quavering lip until they closed the door behind him and her husband looked back down at her.

"I love you too, you know."

Stephen nodded, then narrowed his beautiful blue eyes. "More than three-cheese lasagna from Ruby's?"

More than life. She nodded, lowering her lashes as he maneuvered Little Ned so he could brush his lips against hers. "I must be crazy."

"Because you finally love me more than Italian food?" he whispered, sounding amused.

"Because I'm wondering how long we'll have to wait before we can start working on another set."

"About as long as I'll have to wait to spank you for teasing me like that in front of the babies."

This moment had been worth it. Every discomfort. Every day in bed and every frustrated tear had led to this. To them. Stephen, Ned and Patrick "Huck" Finn. Her boys. Like Seamus, she'd gotten so much more than she'd ever expected for Christmas. She'd just had to wait until January to open her gifts.

**Turn the page for more
Finn Factor books!**

THANKS FOR READING!

I truly hope you enjoyed this book. If so, please leave a review and tell your friends. Word of mouth and online reviews are immensely helpful to authors and greatly appreciated.

If you love the ***Finn Factor*** series and want to hang out with like-minded others, as well as get access to exclusive discussions, contests and prizes join THE FINN CLUB on Facebook:)

To keep up with all the latest news about my books, release info, exclusive excerpts and more, check out my website RGAlexander.com. Friend me on Facebook to join for contests, and smutty fun.

Friend me on **Facebook**
https://www.facebook.com/RGAlexander.RachelGrace

The Finn Club
https://www.facebook.com/groups/911246345597953/

CHECK OUT *Curious,*
BOOK 1 OF THE FINN FACTOR SERIES

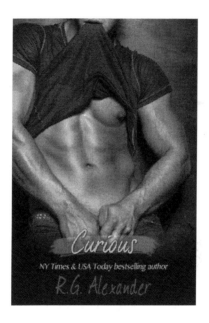

"Everyone go buy the f***ing thing. Curious. Go now." tweet
by author of Love Lessons,
Heidi Cullinan

"When I got to the end of this book, I wanted to start over…
RG Alexander is one hell of an author!"
USA Today bestselling **Bianca Sommerland**,
author of Iron Cross, the Dartmouth Cobras

Are you Curious?

Jeremy Porter is. Though the bisexual comic book artist
has known Owen Finn for most of his life—long enough
to know that he is terminally straight—he can't help but
imagine what things would be like if he weren't.

Owen is far from vanilla—as a dominant in the local fetish community, he sees as much action as Jeremy does. Lately even more.

Since Jeremy isn't into collars and Owen isn't into men, it seems like his fantasies will remain just that forever...until one night when Owen gets curious.

Warning: **READ THIS!** Contains explicit m/m nookie. A lot of it. Very detailed. Two men getting kinky, talking dirty and doing the horizontal mambo. Are you reading this? Do you see them on the cover? Guy parts will touch. You have been warned.

Available Now!
www.RGAlexander.com

Big Bad John
Bigger in Texas series, **Book One**

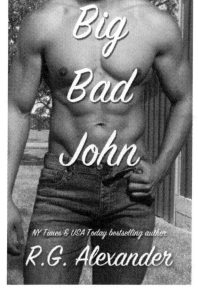

Available Now!
www.RGAlexander.com

Kinda broad at the shoulder and narrow at the hip…

Trudy Adams never planned on going home again. Not to that sleepy little Texas town where everyone knew her business and thought she was trouble. She ran away to California years ago, and now, after what has felt like a lifetime of struggling, her lucky break might finally be around the corner.

And then she got that email.

John Brown has been waiting patiently for Trudy to return, but his patience has run out. He's had years to think about all the things he wants to do to her, and he's willing to use her concern for her brother, her desire to help her best friend get her story, and every kinky fantasy Trudy has to show her who she belongs to.

The explosive chemistry between them is unmistakable. But will history and geography be obstacles they can't overcome? When Trouble makes a two-week deal with Big Bad...anything can happen.

Warning: **READ THIS!** BDSM, explicit sex, voyeurism, accidental voyeurism, voyeurism OF voyeurism with a sprinkle of m/m, exhibitionism, ropes, cuffs, gratuitous spanking, skinny dipping, irresponsible use of pervertables...and a big, dirty man who will melt your heart.

BILLIONAIRE BACHELORS SERIES

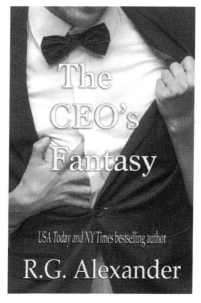

Available Now!
www.RGAlexander.com

Glass slipper shopping can be a dangerous pastime…

The CEO's Fantasy-Book 1

Dean Warren is the billionaire CEO of Warren Industries. He's spent the last five years proving his worth and repairing his family's reputation. But the rules he's had to live by are starting to chafe, especially when it comes to one particular employee. He doesn't believe in coincidence, but when Sara Charles shows up suddenly unemployed and asking him to agree to a month of indulging their most forbidden fantasies--there's no way he can refuse.

When reality is better than his wildest dreams, will the CEO break all of his own rules to keep her?

The Cowboy's Kink-Book 2

Tracy Reyes is a man who enjoys having control. Over his family's billion dollar land and cattle empire, over the women he tops at the club, and over his life. When teacher Alicia Bell drops into his lap with a problem that needs solving and a body that begs to be bound, he can't resist the opportunity to give her the education in kink she needs. But can he walk away from his passionate pupil when it's time to meet his future bride?

The Playboy's Ménage-Book 3

Henry Vincent and Peter Faraday have been friends forever. The royal rocker and polymath playboy have more than a few things in common. They're both billionaires, they both love a challenge...and they've both carried a long-lasting torch for the woman that got away. Finding Holly again brings back feelings and memories neither one of them wanted to face. But they'll have to if they want to share her. Keeping her from running again and making her admit how she feels about them will take teamwork. Hours of teamwork...and handcuffs.

The Bachelors

We know every debutante's mama wants a piece of their action, but if you could choose without repercussions, which of the Billionaire Bachelors would be your fantasy? The true hardcore cowboy who has enough land and employees to start his own country, but no dancing partner for his special kind of two-step? The musician with a royal pedigree, a wild streak and a vast fortune at his disposal, who's never been seen with the same woman twice? His best jet-setting buddy who can claim no less than five estates, four degrees and three charges of lewd public behavior on his record? Or the sweet-talking, picture-perfect tycoon-cum-philanthropist who used to be the baddest of the bunch but put those days behind him when he took over as CEO of his family's company? (Or did he?)

Pick your fantasy lover--rocker, rancher, rebel or reformed rogue. Glass slipper shopping is a dangerous sport to be sure, especially with prey as slippery as these particular animals, but I'll still wish all my readers happy hunting.

From Ms. Anonymous
Available Now!
www.RGAlexander.com

OTHER BOOKS FROM R.G. ALEXANDER

Fireborne Series
Burn With Me
Make Me Burn
Burn Me Down-*coming soon*

Bigger in Texas Series
Big Bad John
Mr. Big Stuff-
Big Trouble-*coming soon*

The Finn Factor Series
Curious
Scandalous
Dangerous
Ravenous
A Curious Wedding
Shameless
Fearless
Lawless

Billionaire Bachelors Series
The CEO's Fantasy
The Cowboy's Kink
The Playboy's Ménage

Children Of The Goddess Series
Regina In The Sun
Lux In Shadow
Twilight Guardian
Midnight Falls

Wicked Series
Wicked Sexy
Wicked Bad
Wicked Release

Shifting Reality Series
My Shifter Showmance
My Demon Saint
My Vampire Idol

Temptation Unveiled Series
Lifting The Veil
Piercing The Veil
Behind The Veil

Superhero Series
Who Wants To Date A Superhero?
Who Needs Another Superhero?

Kinky Oz Series
Not In Kansas
Surrender Dorothy

Mènage and More
Truly Scrumptious
Three For Me?
Four For Christmas
Dirty Delilah
Marley in Chains

Anthologies
Three Sinful Wishes
Wasteland - Priestess
Who Loves A Superhero?

Bone Daddy Series
Possess Me
Tempt Me
To The Bone

Elemental Steam Series Written As Rachel Grace
Geared For Pleasure

About R.G. Alexander

R.G. Alexander (aka Rachel Grace) is a *New York Times* and *USA Today* Bestselling author who has written over 45 erotic paranormal, contemporary, urban fantasy, sci-fi/fantasy and LGBTQ romance books for multiple e-publishers and Berkley Heat.

She has lived all over the United States, studied archaeology and mythology, been a nurse, a vocalist, and for the last decade a writer who dreams of vampires, airship battles and happy endings for all.

RG feels lucky every day that she gets to share her stories with her readers, and she loves talking to them on Twitter and FB. She is happily married to a man known affectionately as The Cookie—her best friend, research assistant, and the love of her life. Together they battle to tame the wild Rouxgaroux that has taken over their home.

To Contact R. G. Alexander:
www.RGAlexander.com
Finn Club
https://www.facebook.com/groups/911246345597953/
Facebook:
http://www.facebook.com/RachelGrace.RGAlexander
Twitter: https://twitter.com/RG_Alexander

Made in the USA
Columbia, SC
09 July 2020